INSECTS ARE JUST LIKE
YOU AND ME
EXCEPT
SOME OF THEM HAVE
WINGS.

INSECTS ARE JUST LIKE YOU AND ME EXCEPT SOME OF THEM HAVE WINGS.

SHORT FICTION BY KUZHALI MANICKAVEL

BLAFT

PUBLICATIONS
PRIVATE LIMITED

Chennai

First printing July 2008
Second printing September 2008

Blaft Publications Pvt. Ltd.
#27 Lingam Complex
Dhandeeswaram Main Road
Velachery
Chennai 600042
email: blaft@blaft.com
website: www.blaft.com

ISBN 978 81 906056 3 2

Acknowledgement is made to the following, in which some of the stories in this collection were originally published, some in slightly different form: *Gambara* (http://gambara.org), "Miraculous"; *DesiLit* (http://www.desilit.org), "Welcome to Barium"; *Subtropics*, "The Dynamics of Windows"; *Salt Flats Annual 2*, "The Butterfly Assassin"; *Caketrain*, "The Unviolence of Strangers"; *Grasslimb Journal*, "You Have Us All Late and Follow"; *The Café Irreal* (http://home.sprynet.com/~awhit/), "Cats and Fish", "Because We Are Precious and Brave"; *Per Contra* (http://www.percontra.net), "The Dolphin King"; *Quick Fiction*, "Spare Monsters"; *The Canadian Writers Collective*, "Hoodoos"; *Smokelong Quarterly* (http://smokelong.com), "Little Bones", "Mrs. Krishnan"; *Cadenza*, "The Sugargun Fairy"; *Shimmer*, "Flying and Falling"; *Farafina*, "Paavai", "Murali"; *Opium Magazine* (http://www.opiummagazine.com), "These Things That Can Happen"; *FlashFiction.net* (http://flashfiction.net), "The Perimeter"; *Edifice Wrecked* (http://www.edificewrecked.com), "The Queen of Yesterday".

Drawings in figures 1, 3, 4, 5 and 6 from *A General Textbook of Entomology* by Dr. A.D. Imms, 1925. Photograph in figure 7 from www.thembugs.com, used with the kind permission of Them Insects, Inc.

Printed in India at Sudarshan Graphics, Chennai

CONTENTS

The Godlet

The minute Malathi takes charge, the universe begins to sing her name like it is something holy. She cracks her knuckles and creates a new day that consists of Sunday morning, Saturday afternoon and Thursday night. There will be no more Mondays. The universe applauds her decision.

·

Malathi's bed sheet thickens around her like a callus and she feels omnipotence race inside her teeth, rustling beneath her scalp. She is infinity in the making, a small, good thing.

A goodlet. A good Godlet.

The light shifts and she glows like a white stone inside her cocoon.

·

Malathi wonders if her superpowers will be lightning bolts or tornadoes, if they will come out of her eyes or her mouth. Her fingers slip between her legs but there is nothing there. She hopes her superpowers are not in her armpits.

·

Footsteps bang against her door. She wills them to be quiet and go away. Bony fingers rip the bed sheet away, revealing a bright, harsh face that bobs above her like an angry balloon.

"What do you think you're doing?" says the balloon. "What the hell?"

Malathi opens her mouth and waits for lightning bolts or tornadoes but nothing happens. She feels her body being rearranged and lifted.

"You can't," says Malathi. "I'm the fucking Godlet."

The floor sways and rolls beneath her softened heels. The universe is not listening to her anymore.

YOU HAVE US ALL LATE AND FOLLOW

At six in the morning, the bus to Neelankarai is brimming with sweaty elbows and old Tamil movie songs. The sun begins to rise over a broken bridge and I curl my fingers away from the window. You can catch anything from a bus window: lice, viral fever, depression, pregnancy. Veena is sitting beside me, leafing through her collection of Unphrases.

"*Drissling Days, Do Not Worry, Walk and Dance, Jump into Jackets,*" she says. "I got that from a bar in Bangalore. It's perfect, don't you think?"

"Perfect for what?"

"For today. Today is such a drissling day."

Neelankarai begins to appear in sporadic patches of bleached buildings and shabby beaches. Everything smells like fish and moist diseases.

"I think Neelankarai means blue sand," I say. "Or blue shores."

Veena rolls her eyes and snaps her notebook shut.

"That is so fuck-all," she says. "Sand is not blue."

"Maybe the water is."

"Water is not blue, it's see-through. Oh my god, that rhymes."

"You should write that down."

When the bus finally stops, beggar children mill around the door, hands outstretched to show the fragile creases of sand that line their palms. It is a common misconception that beggar children want your money. What they really want are your kidneys.

"Akka," says a wiry girl with green eyes. "If you could spare some change..."

"For what?" asks Veena.

"For something to eat."

"And what am I supposed to eat?"

The girl spits and moves on to another bus.

"That was definitely a kidney thief," I say.

"Good thing I don't have any kidneys," says Veena.

•

Neelankarai is littered with crumpled pieces of paper and tiny piles of sand that are trying to escape the beach. We decide to have lunch at Puratchimani's Mess, a weary-looking building that sags under the heat of the afternoon. Mr. Puratchimani sits at the cash register, reading a Communist newspaper.

"*When a Hungry Man Is Sleeping, Don't Wake Him and Say No Food for You,*" says Veena, sifting through her notebook. "I read that in an autorickshaw. It's so apt."

"Apt for what?"

"Apt for me. It's like my tagline."

"You're not a hungry sleeping man."

"Metaphorically I am."

"Right."

"You don't know what a metaphor is, do you?"

"No."

The food is lukewarm and watery, served on a banana leaf which is draped over a stainless steel plate.

"There's a plate under the banana leaf," I say.

"So?"

"*Life Is Like One Lunch with Two Plates.* What do you think?"

"I think there's mold on your leaf, right next to your pickle."

I watch the rice and vegetables collapse into each other and decide that I'm not hungry. When we pay the bill, I notice a fierce sketch of a man painted on the wall outside.

"Who is that? He looks very familiar," I say.

"He's that North Indian freedom fighter," says Veena. "The poet one. Aren't I right, Anna?"

Mr. Puratchimani looks up from the money he is counting.

"That's Che Guevara," he says.

"Right, the poet guy. That Hindi fellow."

Mr. Puratchimani slams his hand down on the table.

"It's Che Guevara! You don't know who Che Guevara is? Aren't you educated?"

"What does that have to do with anything?" says Veena.

"He was a Cuban revolutionary!"

3

"Why would we know anything about Cuban revolutionaries?"

Mr. Puratchimani tosses her his Communist newspaper.

"You can read about him in this. You can also read about our fishermen that keep disappearing in foreign waters. You can read about the kidney rackets that have grown out of control after the tsunami. This country is being raped by its own people!"

"Not me," I say. "I never rape anyone."

"You're both educated citizens of India, aren't you?" says Mr. Puratchimani. "What do you have to say about the raping of your country? What are you going to do about the kidney rackets?"

"Why are they called rackets?" asks Veena. "It makes me think of tennis rackets made out of kidney beans."

Mr. Mani tells us to keep his Communist newspaper and encourages us to get a subscription. As we walk home, the picture of Che Guevara seems to shimmer in the heat.

"Che Guevara," says Veena.

"Are you going to write that down?" I ask.

"No, I just like saying it. CheGuevaraCheGuevara."

•

Our rented room has light green walls, two mattresses and two plastic chairs. The afternoon settles in the corners like bundles of thick wool.

"*A Man Lost His Leg and Many Animals Died,*" says Veena. "That was from a newspaper my lunch was wrapped in once."

"How come I don't *get* any of these?" I say. "What am I not *getting* here?"

"Remember Adhi? He loved this book. Whenever we went out I would read something from it and he would clap his hands and go 'Ha!' It was kind of irritating."

In the evening we walk to the beach because someone told Veena they sold fried fish there. The beach turns out to be hot and empty and nobody is frying anything. The ground is littered with broken sea shells and pieces of glass. There's hardly any sand.

"We are going to get sunstroke and die here," I say.

"Let's sit for five minutes," says Veena. "Maybe they're still fishing or something."

4

YOU HAVE US ALL LATE AND FOLLOW

I scan the horizon, looking for a sunset but I can't find one. A thin, ragged figure is walking along the beach towards us.

"Kidney thief," I whisper and clamp my arms securely against my sides. "I heard they bite. Imagine losing your kidneys and getting rabies at the same time."

"Did I ever tell you about the time I was on the bus and this baby leaned over and bit my arm?" says Veena. "I whacked it, *phut,* right on the nose. That's a golden rule—whenever something bites you, whack it on the nose."

The kidney thief is spitting as she walks. I try to keep track of where she spits so I won't step in it afterwards.

"You there, do you know where they sell the fried fish?" asks Veena.

The kidney thief stops and spits in the sand.

"No fried fish here," she says.

"Someone told me there was."

"Nope," she says and spits again.

"Stop spitting like that, for God's sake!" I say. The kidney thief yawns and stretches out her hand in a half-hearted way.

"Haven't had anything to eat, Akka," she says.

"What a coincidence," says Veena. "Neither have we. So you're actually begging from two hungry people. How do you think that will work out for you?"

The kidney thief makes a rude gesture and disappears down the beach.

"Do you remember where she spat?" says Veena. "I don't want to step in it when I get up."

We can't remember so we turn around and get up because we are pretty sure she didn't spit behind us.

•

At night the ocean sucks all the oxygen out of Neelankarai. We sit in our doorway and have curd and mango pickle for dinner because it is too hot to eat anything else. Veena leafs through her book, underlining and highlighting.

"Do you ever cross anything out?" I ask.

"Of course not," she says. "What would be the point of that?"

"You should have written down what I said at lunch."

"What did you say?"

"I can't remember. Something about lunch on two plates."

That night I dream I am standing in front of Puratchimani's Mess, which is slowly sinking into the sand. The kidney thief is standing on the roof.

"Thank you all for coming," she says.

"I have a question," I say. "Why do you keep spitting all the time?"

"On this very special occasion, we want to thank you for giving us all of your kidneys."

"I didn't give you my kidneys!"

"Yes you did. You said you didn't know what to do with them and they didn't fit you anyway."

The kidney thief holds out a banana leaf filled with broken seashells and pieces of glass.

"What's that?" I ask.

"Your kidneys."

"Aren't they supposed to look like beans?"

"As a token of our appreciation, we would like to present you with a special something."

The kidney thief unfurls a newspaper and clears her throat.

"*You Have Always Been Late*," she reads.

"What?"

"It works better if you write it down. Write it on your hand or something."

"I don't have a pen."

"I'll repeat it if you like. *You Follow and Make Us Late All the Time.*"

"That's not what you said the first time."

"Write it down, why aren't you writing this down?"

Puratchimani's Mess sinks deeper into the sand, burying the kidney thief up to the neck.

"*You Follow* what?" I ask. "What did you say?

The sand shudders and heaves, swallowing the kidney thief along with Puratchimani's Mess.

·

When I wake up it is past noon. Veena is eating the last of the curd, which has gone so unbelievably sour I can smell it from across the room.

"I got something for your book," I say.

Veena fishes out a piece of mango pickle from the bottle and pops it in her mouth.

"Well?" she says.

"*You Have Us All Late And Follow*."

Veena's jaw flicks from side to side, as if she is rolling the words around her tongue.

"Well?" I ask.

"Say it again."

I close my eyes and try to remember the exact words. I suddenly wonder if I was supposed to save the kidney thief. I wonder if my kidneys brought her bad luck.

"*I Will Follow You Always, Even When You Are Late*," I say.

"That's not what you said."

"Something something following and being late," I say. "I can't really remember."

I have a feeling today will be marked by large and extraordinary things. I decide that if I see the kidney thief, I will let her have my kidneys.

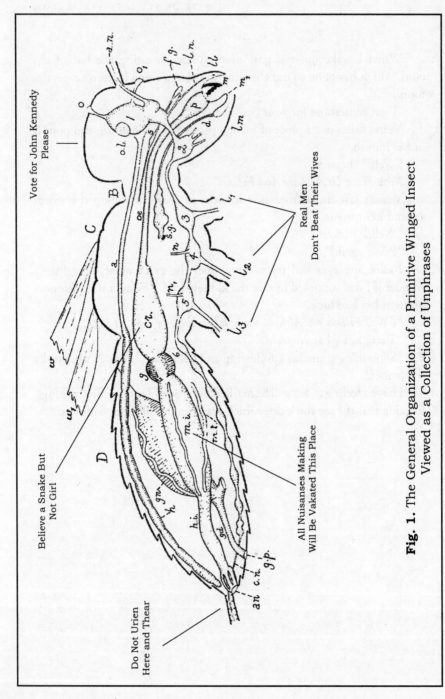

Fig. 1. The General Organization of a Primitive Winged Insect
Viewed as a Collection of Unphrases

Vote for John Kennedy
Please

Believe a Snake But
Not Girl

Do Not Urien
Here and Thear

Real Men
Don't Beat Their Wives

All Nuisanses Making
Will Be Vakated This Place

8

PAAVAI

When Paavai's husband was found face down in the river, she realized that death really *was* like a door closing. Almost immediately, he began to harden in a corner of her heart like a petrified seed. The women took their hair down and wailed, grasping at Paavai's shoulders as if to remind her that she was still here, even though he wasn't.

"He's gone," they cried and Paavai thought of how he was gone and yet he was there, draped in garlands and questions that everyone was making up the answers to.

·

She knew she would dream of him because that was what happened when husbands died without telling their wives—they came back to explain themselves. A few nights later he appeared with water flowing from his hair and lips. She poked him in the chest and felt her finger sink in.

"Does that hurt?" she asked.

"Not so much."

"You needn't come again. What's done is done. And I don't like dreaming about dead people."

"Alright," he said and appeared again the next night.

"What did you do with my watch?" he asked.

"I buried it."

"Why didn't you keep it?"

"This is very distressing for me, you said you wouldn't come anymore."

"This is the last time."

"Promise?"

"I promise."

•

When he was alive, Paavai's husband seemed to fill the entire hut, his shoulders and chest pressing against the ceiling like a pot of rising batter. Now he seemed to be filling her head every time she closed her eyes. She felt like cracking open her skull so she could let him out.

"Why can't you leave me alone?"

"Why did you bury my watch, I don't understand."

She put her hand on his chest and felt her fingers disappear.

"Don't come back," she said. "If you do I will—"

"You will what?" he said. "What will you do?"

She watched as her hand slowly sank into his chest.

•

One night Paavai dreamed the hut was on fire and all she had to save it was a tumbler of water. He appeared beside her. She tried to wring the water out of his elbows but her fingers kept sinking into him.

"Help me to understand why you would bury a watch," he said. "Why didn't you keep it?"

"Why should I?"

"Because it was mine."

"What does that matter?"

They stood and watched as the hut fell over with a half-hearted grunt. There were no sparks, no smoke. It was as if someone had turned off a light.

"Were you serious when you told me not to come anymore?" he said.

"Yes."

"I thought you were joking."

Paavai pulled her fingers out of his arm and tossed the tumbler on the ground.

•

The next morning Paavai dug up her husband's watch—it looked shiny and out of place in the ground, as if someone had lost it. She tucked it into the hip of her sari and walked to the river where he had drowned. For some reason she expected him to be there, face down and bloated like a rotten balloon.

Paavai tossed his watch into the water and watched it sink.

Ezekial Solomon's Shoe

Twelve years after Ezekial Solomon went missing, his shoe appeared in the middle of the road, right outside Iyengar's Bakery. Rolled inside the toe was a moth-eaten tie, two banana spiders* and a shiny brown centipede that sparkled in the sun.

"What should we do?" asked Seshadri. He somehow felt responsible because the shoe had been found outside his bakery and he used to sit in front of Ezekial when they were in school.

"Bury it," said the mailman so Seshadri went to the back and buried it, placing a drooping red shoeflower on top of the freshly-turned soil. The next morning it was back in front of the bakery, complete with the tie, banana spiders and the centipede.

"Oh dear," said Seshadri because he was afraid something like this might happen.

"Keep it," said the mailman.

"But I don't want it. You take it."

"I don't want it either."

Seshadri put it back in the middle of the road and decided to pretend it wasn't there.

•

Right before Ezekial had disappeared, he had turned and waved at Seshadri, who was standing at the bus stop. Ezekial had walked up to him, wearing three old coats, two pairs of trousers and a collection of ties around his head. Hanging around his neck was a black shoe and a brown boot.

---

* This is a South Indian English name for *Heteropoda venatoria*, a spider related to those known elsewhere as huntsman or giant crab spiders.

"Do you like it?" asked Ezekial, sticking out his wrist. He had covered it with silver foil from a cigarette pack. "My new watch."

"Very nice. What time is it?" asked Seshadri.

Ezekial frowned at his wrist, shook it out and then pressed it to his ear.

"It's o'clock time," he said with a grin.

"Won't you lend it to me?"

"No," said Ezekial, shaking his head.

"Give me a tie then."

"No, I need them."

"All of them?"

"Yes." Ezekial began to carefully count the ends of the ties, then his fingers and his ears.

"Give me your shoe."

Ezekial frowned thoughtfully and nodded.

"I'll do one thing. I'll give you a tie and shoe when I'm finished."

Ezekial began striding away, bobbing up and down like he was wading through waist-deep water. Then he turned, waved at Seshadri and vanished.

·

For a while, people wondered where Ezekial had gone. Sometimes they would lounge in front of the bakery, musing about the logistics of being hit by a bus or getting bitten by a snake.

"What do you think Seshadri?" they would say and Seshadri would shrug.

"Maybe he just disappeared," he would say. Most people would chuckle at this but a few would nod as if it was entirely possible.

Once a week, Seshadri would slowly walk the road where he had seen Ezekial disappear. He would frown at the cracks and poke at them with his toe, his head slightly averted in case something happened. Sometimes he would tramp along the sides, looking for a brown boot or one of Ezekial's old coats. Once he found something that looked like the end of a tie—he was about to pick it up when someone passed and asked what he was doing. He came back for it a few days later but by then it was gone.

One year, when the rains had been very heavy, the roads flooded and water the colour of strong coffee flowed past the bus stop. Men crowded around the entrance of the bakery, moodily chewing on buns, giving a running commentary on the debris that floated past. A bright blue door gently wafted along the brown water and four men rushed out to save it because there was nothing better to do. A dog was pulled from the water only to die a few hours later behind the bakery. A stout black pig swam stubbornly upstream and looked like a tiny black island in the water. After unsuccessfully trying to pull it to safety, the men hooted and egged the pig on.

"That's the way! Keep going, keep going!"

Seshadri stood with them, watching rotted sticks, plastic bags and dried coconuts float past. Then he saw a strip of silver foil skipping along the surface of the murky water. It was curved like a sloppy half-moon, like someone had molded it to their wrist, pointed at it and said it was o'clock time.

"There!" shouted Seshadri. A young man who was very keen on saving something from the flood was already in the water, his trousers rolled above his knee.

"What?" said the young man. "Who? Who?"

"There!" said Seshadri. His right leg was in the water though he hadn't rolled up his trousers yet. He felt something warm and gentle touch his foot, then slither away. The sun slid onto the horizon from under a thick cloud and the coasting, brown water seemed to flow into a sheet of blinding, white light.

"Who?" called the young man. "What was it? What did you see?"

Seshadri squinted at the horizon then took another step forward. The water seemed to be encrusted with a crumpled layer of silver foil. He stared at it, feeling his eyes water and burn.

"It was nothing," he said, wading back to the side of the road.

"It must have been something," said the young man. "Something must have made you come charging into the water like that."

"No, it was a mistake," said Seshadri heading back into the bakery. "I didn't see anything."

Ezekial Solomon's shoe was now sitting in the middle of the road, pointing towards the bus stop like someone had left it behind in mid-sprint. Seshadri's plan to pretend it wasn't there worked in sporadic fits and starts. He angled his chair away from the road and arranged a few jars of butter biscuits to obscure his vision. Then he suddenly found himself wandering towards the entrance, stretching and shaking out his legs, his eyes immediately latching on to the shoe. He went back to his table and read the paper twice, then struck up a conversation with a patron who turned out to be partially deaf but had a zest for talking nonetheless.

Sometime during the afternoon, a well-meaning citizen picked up the shoe and tossed it to the side of the road. It landed right in front of Iyengar's Bakery; Seshadri looked at it, rubbed his face and sighed. He picked up the shoe and knocked out the centipede and banana spiders.

"Don't come back," he said, as he watched them scuttle away into cracks in the ground.

He kept the shoe under his table, beside an old biscuit tin that had rusted shut. Every so often, he would tap it with the side of his foot, to make sure it was still there.

WELCOME TO BARIUM

We Are Honoured By Your Journey

You have reached the heaviest place on earth—a fine, upstanding building filled with exploding women, bordered by courageous trees. Please be alert. The third-floor residents like to throw things out the window. It smells because that's what happens when you put InsideOut women and UpsideDown women under the same roof. They expand and contract, poke into corners, stretch into the floor. They get squished against each other, rupture and bleed, overflow and dry up. They have a tendency to ignite because that is the elemental nature of exploding women. They also love to dance and clap their hands.

Rubber Band Girls and Super Queens

"So where were you yesterday?" asks Rudra. Rudra is a repeat customer. She began as an ordinary Rubber Band Girl, stretching and sighing, screaming and soiling herself. A few weeks ago she was crowned Super Queen after she jumped the wall and ran to the bus stop with slices of glass stuck in her heel. This conclusively proved that she would expand and contract until she finally snapped.

"Do you think you are very beautiful?" she asks. Last Saturday, Rudra insisted that you *were* very beautiful but Super Queens have a set of rules that are subject to change without notice. Rudra doesn't mind drinking your abandoned coffee either, even though it's been sitting there for the last hour and is covered in red ants. She stirs it with her finger and you wonder if the ants aren't biting her or perhaps she just doesn't feel them.

"I don't think you're beautiful," she continues thoughtfully. "I can see your arrogance all over your face. And your mouth is crooked. You're not beautiful at all."

You wish Rudra was on the third floor, soaked with meds, her mouth hanging open like an empty bag. She smiles at you and takes a sip of your coffee. You watch the ants swarm around her lips and wonder if they aren't biting her or perhaps she just doesn't feel them.

Chemical Candy

Dr. J.J. Shiv Shankar wears his black silk shirt to work because he wants everyone to know that he's a Dancing Machine. He likes it when he walks in and the girls smile appreciatively and sing *"Jai Jai Shiva Shankar, Kaanta Lage Na Kankar"*. It gives him a chance to wiggle his thin hips in the reception area. He is very resourceful and likes to try new things, especially free samples. His crowning achievement is the blue tablets that made all the exploding women walk backwards.

"It was very clear," he will tell you, "that they wanted to move forwards. But for some reason, they kept walking backwards, even though they had their arms outstretched, like they really, really wanted to move forwards."

There Once Was a Girl Named

The phone rings and you pick it up because you're the only one here and you're bored.

"There's a crazy person at the Chepet bus stand."

"Ma'am we can only help if it's a woman—"

"Yes! Yes, she's a woman and she's spitting at people and lifting up her sari and she's got worms crawling out of her arm and she's spitting—"

"Has she been violent?"

"She's spitting! For God's sake, she spat on my foot, she—"

"Do you know how long she's been there?"

"I don't know, I—can't you come? Can't you take her?"

"Do you think you could stay near her, just till we get there?"

"What if she spits at me again?"

An hour later a girl who looks like a broken stick is sitting across from you, having the maggots removed from her arm.

"Name?" you say, as you start a new file.

"Didn't say," says the attendant girl.

"Where's she from?"

"Didn't say. She didn't say anything. Let's name her something, how about Reshma? Just for now, R-E—"

"We'll call her Minnal."

"Minnal? Minnal…ok, Reshma Minnal then."

"Minnal Reshma."

"Ok…" says the attendant, though she really doesn't think much of the name Minnal.

Hi Everybody! My Name's Marcus!

Marcus came from America last week, armed with enthusiasm and a backpack of bottled water. Nobody is sure why he is here but he has a PowerPoint presentation and a file folder. Marcus is not as enthusiastic as he used to be because it's so damn hot, his skin is peeling and he has already had two cases of food poisoning. Worst of all, somebody, most likely Rudra, has stolen all his water bottles. Today however he has a plan. He is going to get organized, create modules and have something done by the end of the day.

"So, is there a computer I could use around here?" he asks.

"There's this one," you say, stifling a yawn.

"Great, could I—"

"It shuts down every five minutes though."

"Why?"

"We don't know."

Marcus is momentarily deterred but only momentarily. He grins and shows you his very white, very straight teeth.

"Why don't you let me try anyway, I'm good with computers."

You move but don't get up because Marcus can only have the computer, not the chair. You put your head down, pretending to catch up on some much needed sleep while Rudra quietly stations herself behind Marcus. She is fascinated by his blonde hair and the way his skin turns pink when he goes out in the sun. You count off the seconds with small taps of your hand, hear the telltale beep and open one eye to see Marcus staring in disbelief at the screen.

"What the—" he says. You notice Rudra is smiling because whatever Marcus just said sounded exactly like *otha*, the Tamil word for fuck.

"*Otha,*" says Rudra with a bright smile and Marcus turns to her.

"Hey!" says Marcus.

"*Otha!*" says Rudra.

"Yeah, what the hell, eh?" he says pointing at the computer.

"*Otha nayee!**" says Rudra. "*Otha Marcus!*"

"Yeah, Marcus wants to know what the hell is going on with the computer!"

"*Otha thevidiya payan!***" she says, clapping her hands.

"What the hell, eh?" says Marcus. "What the hell?"

Rudra starts shouting "*Otha!*" repeatedly at the top of her lungs and has to be physically removed. Marcus doesn't understand what has happened.

"What's the big deal? We were just—OH FOR CHRIST'S SAKE!" says Marcus as the computer beeps quietly and reboots.

We'll Send You a Postcard When We Get There

In an obscenely expensive coffee house near the heart of the city, Dr. J.J. is buying you and Marcus lattes because Marcus didn't believe lattes existed in Chennai.

"It's alright," says Marcus. "Not like the ones in New York. You should have a latte in New York."

---

*   "Fucking dog!"
** "Fucking prostitute's son!"

"I'll do that the next time I go there," you say and Dr. J.J. smirks into his Madras filter coffee.

"Guess who took off yesterday," he says.

"Rudra."

"Nope. Maggot Girl."

You remember she shuffled her feet and spat if you came too close. You wonder if she will get maggots again.

"She had a name…," you say and Marcus suddenly looks up from his latte.

"Min..nie..Ray," he says. "Mini Ray… man."

You think of what happens to broken girls whose eyes cannot focus and who pee on their feet. Marcus suddenly slams his hand down on the table.

"It was Krishna. Mini Krishna."

Two days later news arrives that Maggot Girl has been found completely naked and completely dead by the side of the highway. It is only when you open her file that you remember what her name was.

Inhale. Exhale.

You are sitting in a corner, practicing how to breathe—inhale, exhale, inhale. It's been one week since Rudra the Super Queen made her trimillionth escape. Minnal Reshma has been cremated and Marcus has been given a plastic replica of the Taj Mahal as a farewell present. They are beginning to fade like faces in a burning photograph and you think that maybe it's the weight around here that makes people sink. You feel a thickening spread over your blood vessels, your lungs, your bones. You wish you could remember what Minnal's hands looked like, whether her ears were pierced. You wish that maggots would stay out of people's arms and that everyone knew how to close their mouths.

You walk over to the window, stick your head out as far as you can and you inhale.

You exhale.

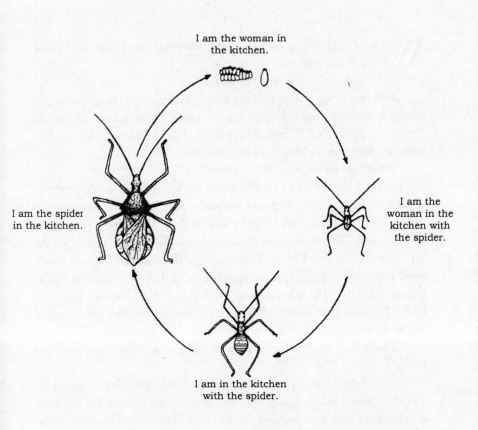

I am the woman in
the kitchen.

I am the spider
in the kitchen.

I am the
woman in the
kitchen with
the spider.

I am in the kitchen
with the spider.

Fig. 2. The Progression of Insanity in Women
Represented by the Life Cycle of the Assassin Bug

Some Singular Event

We have been falling for two weeks, three days, seventeen hours and forty-seven minutes.

"Keep your eyes peeled boys; eyes peeled!"

The crew is very helpful. They keep our windows clean, point out things of interest, remind us to take out our cameras and say cheese. When we all say "Oh!" they always smile, like they completely understand us. So far everything has been real swell.

"What's the report, boys? What's the report?"

It's the Captain who's been driving my companion crazy. Initially, when the Captain said *"Keep your eyes peeled boys,"* my companion would smash his nose against the window so I couldn't see a thing. When the Captain said *"What's the report?"* his hand would shoot up and he would say "Oh-oh! Oh me! Pick me!" Initially he thought the Captain was a swell guy. Now the Captain makes him gnash his teeth and say "Jesus Christ, what the hell? What does he think this is? Is he for real? What the hell?" This strain has unsettled his stomach and frayed his nerves. Even if he thinks a tiny gnashing thought, it undoes him completely.

"C'mon boys, what's the report? Tell it like you see it boys, keep your eyes peeled!"

There is a wheeze, a pop and my companion's tooth lies on my lap in a pool of jellied blood. I pick it up and give it back to him. He swallows it sadly and I hear the clink and settle as it joins the rest of his teeth at the bottom of his stomach.

"Say, why don't you take out your camera?" I say in an effort to cheer him up. "C'mon, take a look at that colour. Just look at that."

The outside is breaking and streaking in purple, blue, orange and green. The crew points and a group of voices say "Oh!" because it's just like the brochure, the commercial and what everyone said it would be like. The crew smiles and nods.

"Look, red! Did you see the red? You should have taken a picture," I say.

My companion shakes his head and sighs. It's no good.

"Tell me a story," he says. "Tell me about that girl you were lonesome for."

A thick streak of white shoots past the window and somebody in the back hoots and whistles.

"Well I started feeling lonesome for her after she died. So I brought her home and she wailed, right?"

"Yeah," says my companion with a yawn.

"So she kept wailing—wouldn't stop until I gave her something to eat. Then she stopped. Then she was quiet and everything was beautiful."

"Is that the end?"

"No."

"So what happened?"

"She ate my watch."

"Look alive there boys, look alive!"

A thick smudge of black pours across the windows and a chorus of groans echo from behind. The crew still smiles, as if they understand our disappointment and wish they could do something about it.

"You should've taken that picture," I say. "Red is a very rare thing to see nowadays."

My companion wheezes as the lights dim. The crew scuffles and sweeps, their eyes peeled like luminous pearls, their smiles glowing like tiny white worms.

The Sugargun Fairy

Even as a child, Stalin Rani bore a striking resemblance to brown wrapping paper. Her body was flat and foldable, her face littered with creases that curled into different shapes when she stood in the sun. Her birth had been celebrated with the bursting of four small firecrackers, three of which never went off.

She began life by crawling along the sagging walls of her house, poking her toes into corners and listening to her father climb the ranks of the local Communist Party. In the afternoons she sat under a table and assigned colours and shapes to the different voices she heard. Some were dark grey and hard like wet cement. Others were oily and brownish-orange like stale halva.

When she was six, a tall twitchy man named Shoebox Uncle came from London to stay with them. He had a broken jaw and a grubby mess of gauze that was wound around his face like a scarf. He completely ignored Stalin Rani's existence and spent most of his time listening to an old radio. Then one day he turned to her.

"You have a terrible name—what is it again, I have forgotten."

"Stalin Rani."

"Queen Stalin. That's almost an oxymoron. Do you know what an oxymoron is?"

"No."

"Do you know what a moron is? Your father, for example, is a moron for naming you Stalin Rani."

"Were you really in London?"

"Why, were you?"

"What was it like?"

"London was filled with rain and sugarplum fairies. They had runny skin and carried pink candy guns around their necks. Every Sunday

I would go out and collect them in my shoebox. Sugarplums with sugarguns. Say it, sugarplums with sugarguns."

"Sugarflums with sugargums."

"Sugarguns with sugarguns. Here," he said, shoving a thick black shoebox into her stomach. "If you ever find any, you can keep them in this."

The box smelled like wood and old honey. Stalin Rani pictured tiny fairies crouched in the corners, their skin puddling into pools between their toes. She imagined them waiting for the lid to fall back so they could shoot Shoebox Uncle in the jaw.

•

The shoebox contained endless possibilities and Stalin Rani often thought of the things that could be inside if they had the chance. She saw it brimming with sharpened purple pencils or yellow frogs with legs that kept getting tangled together. Sometimes she imagined it filled with milk white erasers stacked like bricks. One day she discovered a tiny wing inside.

"Is this from a Sugargun fairy?" she asked, holding it out on her forefinger. Shoebox Uncle frowned and twitched.

"Can't be sure. Put it in your mouth."

Stalin Rani placed it on her tongue and a sour pinprick ran through her teeth.

"Is it like a spoonful of sugar?" he asked.

She shook her head.

"Can you say supercalifragilisticexpialidocious? Backwards?"

"No."

"Then it was probably from a fly," said Shoebox Uncle.

•

The next morning Stalin Rani awoke and the universe stretched over her eyes like a piece of orange bubble gum. She saw a crack in the cosmic egg, elephants mating in a thunderstorm and a broken toilet. She coughed until something hard and black lurched out of her mouth.

"It's a revelation," said Shoebox Uncle. "Put it in your mouth."

"It came out of my mouth."

"Put it in your shoebox then."

Stalin Rani began bringing one up every morning. Soon the shoebox was filled with them.

"How come you don't have them?" she asked.

"I do, I just don't spit them out."

"Why do I have to keep them in the shoebox? How come I can't just throw them out?"

"Because everyone must keep a box of things they don't understand and can't throw away."

•

The shoebox could only hold so many revelations. At the end of every month, Stalin Rani took them to a nearby canal and tossed them in, one by one. Shoebox Uncle came with her and leaned against the railing cracking his neck, wrists, knuckles and then his neck again.

"Careful you don't hit any fairies," he said.

"I thought you said they lived in London."

"I have a feeling I brought a few over. Something was tugging at the back of my head in the plane."

"Lice."

"Not lice."

"There's this girl Mahalakshmi in my class who had so many lice her mother poured DDT on her head and all her hair fell out."

"You just hit one on the head."

"One what?"

"Fairy. Watch where you're throwing."

Stalin Rani scanned the murky water, looking for an arm or a tattered set of wings. Shoebox Uncle was making a crackling sound with his jaw.

"Is it okay?" asked Stalin Rani. He yawned and frowned.

"I think you gave it a concussion."

•

By the time Stalin Rani started school Shoebox Uncle had taken to sitting in the yard for hours at a stretch, staring at the ground with his mouth open. He showed no interest in her Chinese fountain pen or her collection of gold and silver cigarette foils. On Sundays she would sit on the floor and watch him to see if he was up to something. Sometimes she would poke him in the arm.

"What are you doing?" she would ask.

"I'm catching flies."

"Why?"

"Why not?"

Once she watched a fly crawl along his cheek and climb up the side of his nose. It stretched its hind legs and rearranged its wings while Shoebox Uncle breathed noisily through his mouth. Stalin Rani clapped her hands and the fly disappeared into the white sky like a spot of ink.

After that she stopped watching him.

•

Time passed very slowly in Stalin Rani's house. It collected in the corners and clung to people's heels if they stood in one place for too long. It occurred to Stalin Rani that if she stayed any longer, she too would collect in the corners. Her voice would become colourless and cling to the walls like mold.

After failing the tenth grade and passing her typing exam, Stalin Rani decided to leave. By then she hardly saw Shoebox Uncle at all. He had been relegated to the back room of the house, where he spent most of his time twitching and staring at the floor. When her suitcase was packed she went to his room and poked him in the arm.

"I'm leaving," she said. "Do you want your shoebox back?"

Stalin Rani watched him twitch, first shoulder, then head, then shoulder again. She waited an hour for him to say something.

And then she left.

•

The next three years were spent sharing a room with a spider-like girl named Malli and typing out reports in the cramped quarters of Gnanasekaran's DTPXerox and Publics Phone Stall Shop. On weekends she wrote postcards to her uncle that she arranged in chronological order on the bottom of her suitcase. One day a tattered blue envelope appeared under her door. It was from her father.

He said he was pained that she had left so abruptly and hadn't even bothered to call. He was surviving, even though he had so many troubles, the least of which was the humiliation of having a runaway daughter (who he had to track down like a common criminal) but he did not mind because he was only worried about her well-being and hoped she would come to her senses soon and return home.

If she would not come home, would she at least return the shoebox she had stolen from her uncle. It was one thing, he said, to steal from a normal, healthy person. It was quite another to steal from a penniless idiot who was living off the kind-heartedness and generosity of a brother who barely had enough to keep body and soul together. Would she please return the blasted thing because the idiotbastard kept screaming for it like he had demons lodged in his backside and the neighborhood was beginning to think very badly of her long-suffering father.

Or would she send it by post if she was very busy.

•

That night Stalin Rani dreamed of angry claws scuttling and snipping at the door of her old house. Shoebox Uncle was standing in the rain, his eyes covered by two yellow moths. He coughed and the moths fluttered and settled, shaking the rain from their furry backs.

"I asked you," she said. "I asked if you wanted the shoebox back and you didn't say anything."

A puff of tiny, transparent wings flew out of his mouth and hovered in front of Stalin Rani's face. She saw the rain soaking through the moths, dissolving them into streaks of dirty yellow that ran down her uncle's face. That morning there was no revelation—just a thin trickle of black spit crawling down her chin.

•

Malli seemed the most excited about Stalin Rani's trip back home. After ducking out of her house to avoid an arranged marriage, Malli made it a point to visit her home once a month flaunting a handbag and wearing cheap sunglasses.

"Here," she said. "Let those country fruits see that you're a career woman now and you can't be bullied."

The handbag was large and flabby and reminded Stalin Rani of the women she sat beside on the bus. She shoved the shoebox inside and made her way down the stairs to the street.

"Hey!" Malli called after her. "Make sure you come back! That's my only handbag!"

•

Stalin Rani's old house seemed to have stretched in all directions. Balconies and sit-outs had sprouted in awkward corners like pistachio-coloured tumors. Two scooters stood in front of the door and a mess of bicycles lay tangled against the wall. The Communist flag that had hung by the porch for so many years was missing.

"Where's the flag?" she asked as she entered.

"Look at this," said her father, getting up from his reclining chair. "After five years she finally comes to see me and she asks where the flag is—what flag?"

"Have you switched sides?"

"She comes back after seven years and doesn't even ask about my failing health or how I have suffered, barely keeping body and soul together—where are you going?"

"To return his shoebox."

•

Unlike the rest of the house, the backroom seemed to have contracted. The walls that hadn't caved in were being held up by broken furniture and bundles of moldering communist pamphlets. Shoebox Uncle sat in the middle of this, twitching and drooling, his eyes obscured by milky cataracts.

"Here," said Stalin Rani, shoving the shoebox into his lap. He pushed off the lid and ran his fingers over the revelations piled inside. Then he picked one up and began breaking it into small pieces.

"I heard it buzzing," he said. "It's caught in a corner, I think."

Stalin Rani watched the revelations snap between his fingers and wondered why she had never thought of doing that.

"What's caught in a corner?" she asked.

"Can't you hear it?"

"A wasp."

"Don't be an ass," he said and slipped a piece into her limp hand. "Here. See if you can lure it out."

The broken revelation was black all the way through. For some reason she had thought they would be white inside.

"You said I hit a Sugargun fairy when I was throwing these into the canal once, remember?"

"*Plum*. Sugar*plum* fairy."

"You said Sugargun."

"Don't be ridiculous."

"You told me they were called Sugargun fairies."

"I did not, there are no such things as Sugargun fairies. And you killed that one, by the way."

"You said I gave it a concussion."

"You killed it. You made them cry for three nights and four days, I heard them."

Stalin Rani remembered scanning the water and seeing nothing but black algae and cigarette butts. She remembered sleeping away from the window so the fairies couldn't come and beat her with their shiny, angry wings at night.

"It's a wasp," she said, folding the empty handbag into four and tucking it under her arm.

"You didn't even look."

"Yes I did."

"And?"

"It's a wasp."

•

That evening Stalin Rani sat on her bed and tried to remember what her uncle's voice used to sound like when she was younger. She couldn't remember if it was a muffled, sour bread voice or a thin, cracked one that dripped down the walls like a broken egg. She couldn't remember what colour it was either.

She pulled her suitcase out from under her bed and took out all the postcards she had written to him. Their edges were soft and fuzzy—some were already dividing into two or three sheets at the corners. One had separated into five pieces, each curled back and waiting for something to happen.

Stalin Rani opened her window and felt the sunset and purple diesel fumes colour her lips. The evening was settling in a cloak of incense, burning oil and songs that wove in and out of a broken radio. She realized that she had never given Shoebox Uncle's voice a colour at all. Maybe it was something she never got around to.

The postcards fell from the window in soft, jagged pieces, scattering onto the road like flowers on a dirty river.

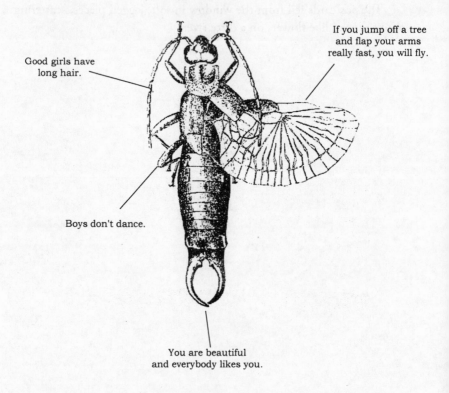

Good girls have
long hair.

If you jump off a tree
and flap your arms
really fast, you will fly.

Boys don't dance.

You are beautiful
and everybody likes you.

Fig. 3. Childhood Mythology Represented as a Male Earwig
with Right Wing Extended

LITTLE BONES

The ice cubes are fuzzy with frost—they were made with monsoon rain which is supposed to be better than ordinary rain.

"Look what I found," I say, holding out the ice tray. Kumar stares at it as if he is looking over the edge of a cliff.

"Those'll make us sick," he says.

"No they won't, they're made out of rainwater."

We spend the morning eating ice and watching tiny green finches spear moths on the window sill.

"I always thought finches ate berries," I say. "They seem too delicate to be carnivorous."

"Is there anything else?"

"What do you mean?"

"Is there anything else to eat besides ice?"

"No."

Kumar puts his glass down and I wonder if he thinks I'm lying.

.

The ice cubes put an edge on the day, making it glow with faint possibilities.

"We should go for a walk," says Kumar. "Or start a garden or something."

I remember how my mother buried fish bones and grocery bills in the backyard because she was scared something would happen if she didn't. Whenever it rained, little bones would poke through the mud like pointing fingers.

"You really want to go for a walk?" I ask. Kumar rubs his face and sighs.

"No, I guess not."

•

Kumar's ice cubes are melting into a scummy pool of water that smells like an old toothbrush. He says there's something crawling along the bottom of his glass but I can't see anything.

"Why didn't you eat them?" I ask. "I ate all mine."

"You're going to get sick."

"I won't get sick, they were rainwater ice cubes."

"Does your tongue burn?"

"A little."

"You're going to get sick."

Kumar gets up, leaving behind a space that hums like angry bees. I watch the last of his ice melt and hear the bones settle into the folds of my skin, the blood crunching in my veins.

Do You Know How to Twist with Girls Like This?

Mira has streamlined down to the shape of a pin. We watch her and wince, muttering about migraines while our eyes click and hum inside our heads.

Did you know, says one of us, that Mira was big-boned as a child? She always had to turn sideways——

you know what I mean, don't you?

She must have taken *extraordinary* measures.

We imagine her shaving down her shoulders and ankles, breaking off what was extra and hiding it in suitcases under her bed.

Later on, someone brought up the possibility of staples.

Are you serious, we grin. What is she holding in?

Well some girls naturally turn into pockets—

it's storage space, really.

Old teeth, pieces of broken soap, people who've whispered to you in a cloud of halitosis.

Things like that.

She's still big-boned then. If you take out the staples. If you look at it logically.

Yes. If you look at it logically, says someone.

We nod and carefully bare our teeth.

KNOWING MAURICE

We were sure that we knew each other; we both had photographs to prove it. But beyond the pictures, it was hard to figure out where or how we had actually met. "Weren't you with that fat fellow—glasses, goatee?" she said. "Always wore a black kurta and jeans?"

"You mean the restaurant chap? The one with the glasses?"

"Restaurant, don't know. Did he have a restaurant? I know he had these glasses, porno-type, thick black frames."

"Right, he brought that Polish girl once, what was her name? Anya? Anoushka? She laughed like she was hiccoughing, remember?"

"Oh you mean that one who stole Amritha's sari."

"She stole Amritha's sari? Really?"

"There was that wedding, remember? Senthil's? And she wanted to go for an Indian wedding in a sari so she borrowed Amritha's and never returned it. That dark blue silk one, Kancheepuram you know."

"Right. Actually I don't think I know Amritha."

"Oh that's a shame, sweet girl. Lovely sari."

"Senthil… that's the stocks chap, right?"

"Right."

"Ok, I—"

"Actually I don't know about the stocks thing but he's in China now. I think. He always came around with the fat fellow, kurta—glasses—don't you remember? He had some firangi name…Michael…Mark…"

"When did Senthil go to China?"

"Maurice! That's the one, Maurice."

"Oh Maurice! Sure, everyone knows Maurice."

"Black kurta."

"Glasses, sure. Crazy bugger."

"I *know*!"

36

"His name wasn't Maurice though."

"Matthew then."

"No..."

"I heard him say 'Some people call me Maurice' once. I remember we were all just sitting there—I think you were there, I'm pretty sure—and he suddenly said that, for no reason. And nobody said anything so I thought he was talking to me."

"Right. Okay, but that's from a song though, isn't it?"

"Really? Is it Rammstein?"

"It's some old band. The Doors. The Jokers...or something."

"I love Rammstein. Don't you? *Büch Dich*."

"Or maybe it was The Beatles. Sounds like something they would sing, no?"

"I know. *Du Hast*."

"I know."

She began rummaging through her purse and I looked at the photograph again. I didn't know who any of them were, not even the one who was supposed to be me.

THE UNVIOLENCE OF STRANGERS

Today's Pavement Piece is crumpled against a bus stop, dying like a freshly-pinned dragonfly. Her mouth is speckled with broken teeth and waves of dust. I never keep my mouth open in the daytime—the heat makes it difficult to swallow.

"Are you hungry?" I ask and wait for a bloodstained finger to crawl out from under her jaw. Perhaps there are moths hanging in silver clusters from the roof of her mouth.

Perhaps she will say something.

.

My grandmother died without saying a word, when nobody was looking. A dog howled and her paper gods fluttered with sorrow inside their makeshift frames. When we lifted her out of her corner, her bones snapped and crumbled like exhausted twigs. Her sari fell away revealing breasts that had collected in sagging puddles of discontent inside her blouse. There was nothing to do except watch the wailing women who passed the time by beating their chests.

.

Today's Pavement Piece stares into the white sky like a freshly-pinned dragonfly. I slip a coin between her broken lips, careful not to touch her.

Perhaps now, she will say something.

BLUE

Blue is the most important. It's not a peacock or turquoise blue. This blue is smoky and dark with whitish-pink flecks in it. It leaves a telltale smudge on the tongue to prove that you've swallowed. It is like the trail of some dark blue fish that has been sent into my stomach to fix my head.

·

I swallow one blue every morning and look defiantly at the upper right hand corner of the room, cheering the little pill on as it tumbles and turns inside me. It's being sent in to straighten things out. Sometimes I hear things being moved into their proper places; I hear the quiet shuffle of thoughts and words being sorted and thrown away. Sometimes I don't hear anything and I have to make up the sounds for myself.

·

I believe this should be a group effort. My elbows, eyelids and fingers need to help too, even if it's just holding a spool of blue thread or collecting blue flakes of paint under my fingernails. I need to absorb all the blue I can get.

Unfortunately I have found that if the blue is smoky it's not dark or if it's dark it's not smoky. If it's smoky and dark it's something like a car or somebody's earring, which I can't touch. However, I have been lucky enough to find a glossy magazine page and a single glove that are a perfect match. My plan is to coordinate the pills, the glove and the paper to work together at the same time. I haven't tried it yet because soaking in all that blue at once might make me explode. Sometimes that thought scares me but usually it doesn't.

·

I cut the magazine page into tiny squares and arrange them in groups of seven. The plan is to eat one square a day, right after the pill. This is nothing like eating paper because I will be placing the squares *under* my tongue. I read somewhere that things are absorbed better that way and even if you put it on your tongue, it's just going to run over the sides and collect on the bottom anyway.

I realize that I haven't figured out what to do with the glove yet—I turn it inside out and notice that it's dirty white inside. I feel cheated and stupid at the same time. Overcome with despair, I eat all the blue squares at once. Nothing happens or maybe something does happen but I don't notice.

·

In the dream there is a bench. Stretching over the bench in an immense arch is a crumbly, blue rainbow. On some occasions it doesn't crumble at all and I tell myself that the blue is definitely working. But usually the rainbow will fall in clouds of blue dust, gently tracing the outline of my feet on the ground.

One day this rainbow will fall down completely.

It is inevitable, like sand castles being eaten by the sea.

THE DOLPHIN KING

At 3 A.M., Senthil is swaying in the middle of the room, talking about Karna. He doesn't know much about the *Mahabharata* but he knows about Karna because he's seen the movie 103 times. If you can improvise a bow and arrow for him along with a voluptuously curved moustache, he will do the entire movie for you, songs included.

"Forget the other guys," says Senthil. "Forget that fucker Arjuna. A hero is someone who knows he's going to be fucked but is heroic anyway."

"What's the point in that?" asks Jameson.

"I mean Karna was better than Arjuna at everything but for some reason we call the sports awards Arjuna Awards. They should be called Karna Awards!" says Senthil.

Once Senthil actually made little Karna Awards out of matchboxes and beer caps. They were supposed to look like trophies but they ended up looking like matchboxes with beer caps stuck to them. Later he found a group of children playing cricket and tried to give them away but nobody wanted them.

"And then he can't die," says Senthil. "There he is, Karna, King Of Everything That Goes Wrong Even When You Do Everything Right, eight million arrows sticking in his chest but he can't die. Just imagine that. I mean just think how much that would hurt."

"Is he from one of those Hindu stories?" asks Jameson.

Senthil blinks as if he's trying to clear his eyes.

"What?" says Senthil.

"This is from one of those Hindu stories, right?"

"Are you kidding me?"

"The *Ramayana* or something?"

"The *Mahabharata*," I say and someone starts to sing the theme song from the *Mahabharata* TV series.

"Get out," says Senthil.

"What?" says Jameson.

"Get out of my house."

This isn't Senthil's house but for some reason Jameson stumbles to his feet and disappears down the stairs—he seems to clatter against the walls and I wonder if he's falling down. Senthil collapses on the floor beside me and I pick bits of popcorn out of his hair and hand them to him. He sadly puts them in his mouth like he's popping pills he knows won't work. An hour later, Senthil decides to go out and buy cigarettes.

"Are you coming back?" I ask.

"Of course I'm coming back. Why wouldn't I come back?"

He disappears down the stairs and I don't see him again for a week.

.

Senthil is a wonderful concept, something that has great potential like a rising sun or a new bicycle. It's only when you take a closer look at him that you notice he's not held together very well. Sometimes he cleans himself up and becomes chubby and irritable, his lips puffing out while his eyes completely disappear into his face. But it's just a matter of time before he starts to wither again; his knuckles and elbows become dry and sharp while his eyes grow like puddles of dark water. You begin to hear stories about how he beat up an autorickshaw in the middle of the road or gave his shoes away to a beggar. Once he called me shortly after news had spread that he had relieved himself on the hood of somebody's Mercedes.

"Guess where I am," said Senthil.

"I have no idea."

"Guduvancherry! I think. It looks like Guduvancherry."

"How did you get all the way over there?"

"Must have taken a train, I think I'm in the railway station—I mean I woke up and there were railway tracks and a tea stall so I'm thinking it's a railway station. I could ask someone if you want—you want to hold on while I ask?"

"Senthil I can't do this now, I'm at work."

"Why don't you come down here? It's very small-townish. I could take you sari shopping. Or we could go to a temple or something."

"I don't think so."

"How come there are no Karna temples around? In all my life I have never seen one Karna temple. I've seen an AIDS manual written in Tamil though. Have you ever seen one of those?"

"Senthil—"

"Did you know they have diagrams? They're not very good ones—I mean I didn't get what they were doing at first and it's hard to make out what the guy is holding. Then you're like oh! Okay, so that's what they're doing. It's strange because she seems to be looking one way and he's looking somewhere else."

"Senthil, I have to go."

"But what's the deal with the Karna temples? Is it against the law to have one?"

"I don't know."

"But then there are no Arjuna temples either. How come none of these guys have temples? I could build one though. I could build a Karna temple, couldn't I?"

"Ok, I'm hanging up now."

"Aren't you coming down here?"

"No."

"I'll wait for you by the weighing machine."

"Hanging up now Senthil."

"I used my last two rupees on this call though."

"So?"

"How am I supposed to get home now?"

The extension tone started to beep and he hung up. I was pretty sure he would spend the day wandering around Guduvancherry, unless of course he wasn't in Guduvancherry in the first place.

•

Senthil usually doesn't visit me because he doesn't like my landlady and my landlady doesn't like him. One day however he shows up with half a candy bar which he ends up eating himself.

"You got fifty bucks?" he asks.

"For what?"

"I'll pay you back."

"I don't have fifty bucks."

Senthil nods and leans against the wall. He suddenly reminds me of a bundle of dead branches that has been sloppily tied together.

"How about if I give you this?" He reaches into his pocket and pulls out a dolphin pendant that has been cleanly snapped in two. "This is Karna. King of the Dolphins."

"Where's the rest of it," I ask.

"A hundred bucks. I'll pay you back."

"Senthil I don't have any money."

He nods and shrugs.

"Keep it then."

"For what?"

"For whatever. In case of something."

After Senthil leaves I try to find a place for the pendant. I don't want to keep it but I don't want to throw it out either. I finally decide to put it outside on the window sill. About an hour later the phone rings.

"It's me," says Senthil. "I stole your sugar tin."

"What?"

"I took your sugar tin when you weren't looking."

"Why?"

"I thought you might have money in it."

"I told you I didn't have any money."

"I thought you were lying. I'll give it back when I see you."

Two weeks later Jameson calls and asks if I will come with him to Central Railway Station. Senthil has called to say he is waiting for us beside some special railway tracks that come from Gujarat.

"Did he go out of town or something?" I ask.

"No," says Jameson. "You know what he did last month? Comes to my house with two fucking geese! Geese!"

"Where did he get geese from?"

"Fuck if I know."

"What did you do?"

"I said fuck off, you can't keep bloody geese in my house!"

Central Railway Station hits us squarely in the nose and we weave through piles of families who have fallen asleep on the floor, boxed in by their luggage. We find Senthil sitting cross-legged on a concrete bench. He holds his arms out, as if he expects us to hug him.

"I wanted you both to see this," he says and gets up. He walks over to the edge of the platform and points down to the start of a railway line. "When the Gujarat riots happened and the earthquake and stuff, people just got on this train and stayed on till it stopped. And this is where it stopped, right here. No more track. This is where they all got off. Isn't that awesome?"

"Oh for God's sake," says Jameson.

"Wouldn't it be awesome to see it stop right here," says Senthil. "And it *will* stop here. Because it can't go any further. There's no more track. I mean where can it go if there's no more track?"

Jameson turns and walks away. I feel I should say something that will change Senthil's life and make him go home.

"Where's my sugar tin?" I ask.

"Your what?"

"My sugar tin. You stole it, remember?"

"What sugar tin?"

I turn and follow Jameson so I can hitch a ride back.

•

Something tangible needs to be done. Something with words and a date and an incident so that years later I can look back and say yes, I told him. Sat him down and said Senthil, drug addicts get raped in the ass and in the mouth. They get pubic lice. Nobody feeds them. They smell bad. But before I have a chance to, Senthil calls up and says he's got a job with a call centre. They are really impressed with him because they think he is dynamic and energetic and they like the way he speaks English. Rumour has it that he will be promoted in a week or so.

We are very proud of Senthil because call centers are easy money. Jameson throws him a party to celebrate and Senthil arrives wearing a long-sleeved shirt that remains buttoned at the wrist for the whole evening. He does however take his socks off and I notice that his big toenails are missing.

"They made me this team leader kind of thing and it's like being in charge of vampires, you know?" says Senthil. "Because we all work at night, right? Karna King of the Vampires."

"I don't think Karna had anything to do with vampires," I say.

"I always think of that song that happens when Karna's trying to die—*Ullathil nallu ullam / Urangaadhenbadhu vallavan vidhithada / Karna varuvadhai yedhirkolladaa.**"

Senthil doesn't sing very well but his Tamil pronunciation is flawless and beautiful like water flowing over rocks. I can sense he is saying something very important, something that could change his life.

A few weeks later, Senthil goes to Mumbai on business and gets fired when he decides he doesn't want to come back.

·

Dreaming of Senthil is inevitable because he is something that intrudes and lingers like a thunderstorm or the tug of a beggar's grubby fingers. When I dream of him, he is standing alone in an abandoned battle field and the sky is a deep, dirty red. He is leaning against a broken pink and yellow chariot, peering into a quiver of moldy arrows.

"Have you died?" I ask.

Senthil frowns and shakes his head.

"No, I don't think so," he says. "They did make me king."

"Who did?"

"They were here a minute ago. I'm pretty sure they said I was king now."

"What are you king of?"

"Eggshells. Fingernail clippings. Broken pencils."

"Dolphins."

"They didn't say anything about dolphins."

"They probably meant to."

"Probably. I feel like I'm probably king of the dolphins too."

Something black is trickling down the outside of the quiver of arrows.

---

*   "The bravest of the brave / Will never rest / This is the law of the mighty / Karna, face what is to come."

I can't tell what it is and wonder if it's really small insects walking in a slow, straight line.

"These arrows burst into fireworks," says Senthil. "Want to see?"

He pulls out an arrow but before he can notch it into the bow it snaps and crumbles to the ground.

"*I had no hope for success,*" I say.

"What?"

"It's a line from the *Mahabharata*."

"Who says that?"

"I don't know. Someone."

"Not Karna. Karna doesn't say that."

Senthil tries to notch in another arrow and it crumbles into his fingers like soot.

"No," I say as the black flecks skitter along the ground and disappear. "Karna doesn't say that."

.

We wait for Senthil to call or mail or do something but nothing happens. Jameson and I begin to consolidate things we have heard about him: he was into event management and had met Deep Purple. He was working with Greenpeace. He was climbing the Himalayas. He was living in a slum and writing a novel. Someone had mentioned seeing Senthil in a railway station, sleeping under a bench but we never talked about that one. Instead we would rearrange the stories slightly or make up something completely new.

Once while we were talking, Jameson took out his wallet and started pulling out his business cards. He began sorting them in different piles, tearing up the ones he didn't need, putting the others in neat stacks of five or six. It seemed like he was making a tiny city of soft, rectangular buildings, neatly cut with straight roads and off-white buildings that had no windows.

"We should go to Mumbai," I said. "We should go see him. Surprise him."

"We should definitely do that."

"Do you have his address?"

"No. Someone will have it though."

"Yeah, someone will."

"He'll probably call us soon anyway. Or he'll just show up, just like that. I think he would probably do that, don't you?"

"He'd probably do that."

I picture the three of us wandering through Jameson's city of cards, turning into the wrong streets, cutting ourselves on the corners, trying to keep in step with people we couldn't see. I think of Senthil sleeping under a bench in a railway station, the King of Things, Karna of the Vampires vomiting on the side of the road, screaming at the buildings for growing in his way and blocking out the sun.

I had no hope for success, I whisper to myself and watch as the pile of ripped business cards grows like a mountain of small mistakes.

Because We Are Precious and Brave

Jobin was leaning against the wall, a bloodied handkerchief against his left eye. He did not seem despondent or in pain—in fact, he looked like he was waiting for the bus. I thought we should probably go to a doctor but Jobin said there was no point, since they had taken his eye with them.

I wondered what they would do with Jobin's eye. Someone said they were artists so there was really no telling what they would do. They would probably wear it in a buttonhole like a chrysanthemum. If they had been animal rights activists they might have given it back.

"D'you know what my grandmother used to say?" said Jobin. "She would say sit in the sun, Jobin. Keep your back straight, think of God and your ancestors blessing you with thick black hair and good eyesight. Everything will be alright."

I pictured Jobin as a small boy, hair neatly plastered to his head, his large, liquid eyes almost too big for his face.

"That's nice," I said.

"Not really. I kept getting sunstroke."

"We could ask for it back you know," I said. "I could take them a cake or a kitten or something. Maybe they've kept it on ice and we can get a doctor to sew it back in. Or maybe it's still in there! Do you think maybe—"

Jobin shook his head and adjusted the handkerchief over his eye. I leaned against the wall and wondered what would be harder—getting his eye back or finding a place to sit in the sun.

Cats and Fish

He stood on the sidewalk pulling small, white cats out of his mouth, each one twisting in his hands like a scorpion caught by the tail. Most of them wandered off, one almost got hit by a car. Another curled up and went to sleep in a flowerpot. He pulled out five cats and then he leaned over and spat into the pavement.

"Hey," I said, though I was sure he wouldn't respond. I said hey to anything—buses, children with ice cream cones, blind people. No one ever said hey back. The man shook his hand like he didn't want anything, didn't have the time.

"Why are you doing that?" I asked.

"Doing what?"

"Pulling cats out of your mouth."

"Why, are you allergic?"

"No."

"Are they bothering you?"

"Not really."

"Want to see something?"

Before I could answer, he began tweezing something out from between his front teeth.

"I think this is yours," he said and held up a tiny goldfish. My fish had died about a week ago but I had left it in the bowl, just in case it wasn't really dead.

"That's not mine," I said.

"Sure it is."

"No, mine was black."

The man looked at the fish and frowned.

"Are you going to do the cat thing again?" I asked.

"No."

"Will you come and do it tomorrow?"

"Don't think so."

I watched as he crumpled the fish into his fist like a piece of paper. I had a feeling that if I had said it was mine, everything would have been different.

THE PERIMETER

It was a completely useless Sunday afternoon. Two girls, A. Lakshmi and B. Lakshmi, were alternately yawning and sighing with boredom. The room was heavy with heat and ennui—even the chairs seemed oppressive. That's when the beetle appeared on the windowsill. The girls eyed it with heavy eyes, slightly resentful that it had the energy to move on an afternoon that spoke of nothing but inertia. It teetered on the ledge and suddenly dropped to the floor with a soft tap. After struggling with the seemingly impossible task of flipping itself upright it began to toddle across the floor. It scuttled up to A. Lakshmi who promptly brought her foot down on it.

"Chee," said B. Lakshmi.

The beetle's abdomen had been crushed, its legs sliding uselessly as it tried to move. A. Lakshmi pursed her lips in disgust and lifted her foot again.

"Wait," said B. Lakshmi.

"It's messing up the floor."

"Why did you step on it then?"

A. Lakshmi rolled her eyes and raised her foot again.

"Wait," said B. Lakshmi.

"Why?"

"It's still alive."

"So?"

B. Lakshmi opened her mouth to say something but decided it was too hot for an afternoon scuffle.

"Whatever," she said, sinking back into her chair.

A. Lakshmi rolled her eyes and gave the beetle a swift kick, sending it skidding into the wall. B. Lakshmi watched as the beetle tried to flip itself upright again. She wanted to help but the thought of getting up was too overwhelming. She should put it back in the garden, under a flower maybe. No, she would put it in a cool, shady place on a huge leaf. It would waggle its antennae back at her and say "Thank you for saving my life." She soon fell asleep, dreaming she was a pink angel in an oppressively hot chair, on a mission to save the squashed bugs of the world.

•

A few hours later, the world was a cooler, kinder place. A. Lakshmi and B. Lakshmi were on the verandah, watching the late afternoon wane into a breathtaking sunset. A solemn, crooked line of ants carried away the remains of the beetle, weaving silently down the porch and into the garden. Neither of them noticed it.

Coconut Water

There is nothing extraordinary about the East Coast Highway—just sand, the scent of decaying fish and the sound of her nylon sari swishing against her ankles. He feels all of this running through his veins like molten electricity, charging through his lips and hands. He closes his eyes and drinks from a dusty, green coconut while a snaking rivulet winds towards his elbow.

She watches him. She pictured this moment when the bus lurched suddenly to avoid a dog. She replayed it over and over again as shabby boys tried to sell her stale tapioca chips and ginger candy. She watches coconut water course down his arm and drip slowly into the sand.

"Was it sweet?" she asks and he nods. She has carried this coconut through two crowded buses—carried it with both hands as if it had a heartbeat.

"Why are you still holding it?" she asks. He feels the sea sparkle and burn into his eyes; the blue sky tightens around his lungs like a fist. He wipes his mouth and lets the empty shell roll from his fingers onto the burning ground.

.

At night the crows fold up like cardboard boxes while moths cling uselessly to the street lamps. He walks briskly, wishing he had marked the place with a stone. He wishes he had put it in his pocket, like a photograph. He runs his fingers through the sand, brushing away hot pieces of broken glass. He finds the empty shell and takes it home, carrying it with both hands as if it had a heartbeat.

2:57 P.M.

Her mouth dissolves into a thin, cold line. I tap my finger on the table, watching as her eyes frost over like icy stones.

"*Just* the margins," I say. "And I'll only use pencil. Promise."

Luckily her intense dislike for me comes with an equally strong need to be polite and accommodating. She slowly extracts her ruler from her box and places it on the neutral area of the bench we share. I already know the rules.

Do not call it a ruler—it is a scale.

Do not put it in your mouth.

Do not use it to scratch yourself.

Do not use it to cut pieces of mango pickle.

When you're finished, give it back. Immediately.

I halfheartedly draw my first margin and turn to her.

"Did you know that your scale is called Dimple?"

I point to the name stamped boldly across the center of the ruler.

"It's an odd name for a rul—I mean a scale. More like a name for…"

I can't think of anything that could convincingly carry off the name Dimple. Out of the corner of my eye I notice that her fists are perched on the table like tiny anxious birds. We have shared this bench for the past six months and I have never touched her hands, not even by accident.

I flip my notebook around, ready to draw the final margin. I can feel her eyes boring into the side of my face—her knuckles have whitened from the strain of waiting. I sigh, place the ruler back on the neutral part of the bench and watch as it disappears behind her thin brown fingers.

I think of the coconut beetles that fly and fall into our house every night like wayward pebbles. I always corner them, hoping they will do something singular and memorable. But they just lie there, the glint of the tubelight ricocheting weakly off their backs.

SPARE MONSTERS

Every day at 4 P.M. we drink coffee at the railway station. We burn our fingers and tongues while the Chennai-Mayavaram Express stretches along the tracks like a dead snake.

"That fraud banana woman asked thirty rupees for a bunch today," says Selva.

"What did you say?"

"I said 'fuck off'. She sells to everyone else for ten."

Selva and I are cursed. We have silhouettes that don't fit anywhere, even though we go to the temple every Friday and have a leaky roof.

"You smell nice," he says.

"It's this medicated soap. I got contact dermatitis."

"You still smell nice."

.

For some reason our house attracts ravens. They settle on the railing like monsoon clouds and don't do anything when we wave our arms and say 'Shoo!' They have stolen five spoons and thrown one of Selva's sandals into the gutter. One day they took our guppies. We point to the empty fishbowl when we tell people about it but nobody believes us.

.

Some nights Selva gets entangled in my hair, his eyes darting back and forth as we listen to the moths swarming at our window. They whisper behind their wings about our white tongues, how coarse and dry our hair is. How we keep blaming the ravens for everything.

"Why are we here?" I ask.

Selva covers my eyes with his hands.

"We're not," he says.

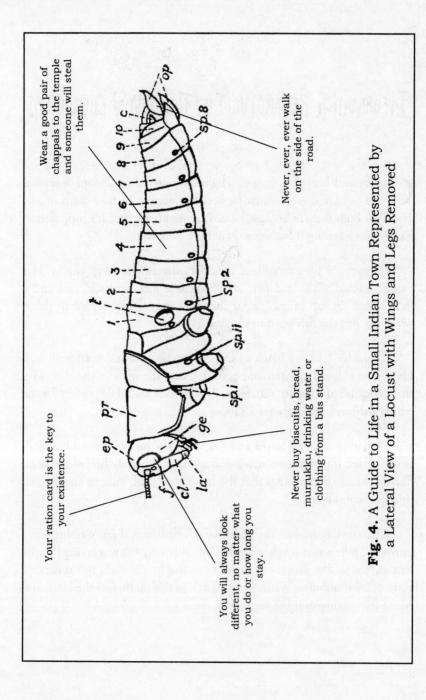

Fig. 4. A Guide to Life in a Small Indian Town Represented by a Lateral View of a Locust with Wings and Legs Removed

Wear a good pair of chappals to the temple and someone will steal them.

Never, ever, ever walk on the side of the road.

Your ration card is the key to your existence.

Never buy biscuits, bread, murrukku, drinking water or clothing from a bus stand.

You will always look different, no matter what you do or how long you stay.

Information Regarding The Two Main Characters

Character 1 keeps his ties and a light bulb on the dashboard of his car. The ties are there because he keeps forgetting to take them inside. The light bulb is there because he can't remember where it's supposed to go. He has a feeling it has been there for a long time.

Character 2 likes to collect imaginary diseases and key chains. Her past is littered with dead pets which include fish, squirrels, cats and a fresh-water shrimp called Caesar that was accidentally boiled to death when she put the fish bowl in the sun.

Character 1 buys a black and white fish because it doesn't look real. He thinks it looks spirited and pixelated and the man in the shop says that's because of its spots. Character 1 believes it would be perfect for the empty fishbowl in Character 2's room.

Character 2 comes home and finds that her lucky bamboo has died. It has rotted into a brown mush and attracted a steady line of red ants. She thinks of all the things that she has named, fed, sang to and stapled into her memory.

Character 1 sits outside Character 2's bedroom door, watching two jumping spiders spar on the wall. He isn't sure why she was crying but she isn't anymore. She promises to come out and he promises to bring her a plate of fried noodles. When he gets back in the car he sees the black and white fish staring in mute surprise at the sky.

MRS. KRISHNAN

I almost wore short sleeves today. It was perfect weather for lemon yellow and green apple, but the sun kept lighting up the scars that run along the inside of my forearm like puckered rivers. They are a tattooed testament to my own laws of physics; a body under immense pressure seeks release through the nearest available wrists. Results may vary—in case of failure, avoid short sleeves.

•

Mrs. Krishnan may have worn short sleeves once, possibly at a friend's birthday when she was in college. She may have powdered her arms but not waxed them. She may have worn a full-length skirt to make up for the inadequacies of her sleeves.

There is a good chance she did not have any scars.

•

Mrs. Krishnan should be sold in little plastic vials at ten rupees a tablet. She is better than Spirulina. She's like super-charged carrots and spinach without the bother of carrots and spinach. She opens the lungs, revitalizes the brain and stimulates blood flow to the heart. No ingestion necessary. Even if you are wasted and useless at the ripe old age of twenty-four, Mrs. Krishnan will make you feel salvageable.

Your sleeves might even go up inadvertently.

•

Mrs. Krishnan is wearing a blue sari today. She looks like she has draped the sea over her shoulder and I tell her so. A black handbag hangs from her arm like a dead crow but I decide not to tell her that. She doesn't seem very talkative today.

Mrs. Krishnan has a son in the States and a husband who wants to take her out for dinner tonight, which Mrs. Krishnan thinks is silly—she tells me this as she combs my hair. She says I should know better than to go out in public looking like a scarecrow. She doubts that I even oil my hair. Then she suddenly wonders if I wash my hair at all.

I guess she is talkative today.

.

My hair is in a tiny braid, my hands are neatly folded on my lap and Mrs. Krishnan is very pleased. She does not tell me I look beautiful because Mrs. Krishnan does not lie—she just says it is good. It inspires her to muse on my future prospects. With such a neatly combed head and well-behaved hands I could resume my studies. Or I could find myself a job and start making some money. Or if I wanted, I could find a nice man and settle down. Mrs. Krishnan is sure that I will find someone though she is not sure where. We both agree we will not find him here.

.

Time always tosses me out before I am ready to go. I am sure I just got here and already I am outside, watching an aggressive bank of dark clouds crowd over the setting sun. I know it will be a damp, gloomy day tomorrow, void of any short sleeve conflicts.

The high point will come at 3:45 p.m. when I will meet Mrs. Krishnan. She will hold my hand and tell me about her son in the States and her husband who wants to take her out to dinner that evening, which she thinks is silly. She will comb my hair and tell me to keep my hands still. Then she will say that I can resume my studies, find a job or find a man—I can do whatever I want.

I look at the sky and realize I have no idea what tomorrow will be like. There is every chance of it clearing up into another short sleeves day.

Monsoon Girls

When Aparna Srinivasan's wedding invitation arrived, Kalai threw it out because she couldn't really remember who Aparna Srinivasan was. Shivani, on the other hand, pinned it to her soft-board at work, took out a piece of paper and began to map out everything she knew about Aparna Srinivasan's existence. She used purple for things she knew had happened and red for things she thought would happen. She called Kalai every half hour to report on her progress.

"She ate bread with curd, remember? And garlic pickle. Bread, curd, garlic pickle, I'm surprised she didn't kill herself. Girls like that *always* kill themselves, it's like having three nipples."

"Who has three nipples?"

"I'm just saying."

"Who are you talking about?"

"Srinivasan, da. College Srinivasan. We should go see her. Don't you want to see her?"

"I'm not sure. Let me think about it and I'll get back to you."

Kalai spent the rest of the afternoon listening to her hands. The heat was making them swell up; she could hear millions of dead seeds and dried tubers jostling against her bones and skin. She fell asleep in her chair and dreamed her hands were huge balloons. They carried her over ships filled with sailors who whistled at her and said *hey girliegirlie*. She tried to whistle back but ended up spitting at them. The sailors started spitting back at her and Kalai wished she had winked at them instead.

•

Kalai decided to join Shivani on her visit because she had nothing better to do. Aparna's house was simmering under the stress of impending nuptials. The small town relatives were seated in the kitchen cutting vegetables while the American relatives were sleeping with their socks on in an air-conditioned room. Aparna's room was dark and forgotten, covered with posters of babies emerging from cabbages or peeping out of watering cans. All of the faces had been plastered over with pictures of leafy green vegetables and light bulbs.

"I feel like dying," sobbed Aparna.

"You're what?" said Kalai.

For some reason Aparna was whispering and Kalai couldn't follow a word she was saying.

"Isn't this the guy you were going out with?" said Shivani.

"So? What difference does that make?" whispered Aparna.

"That's what I thought," said Shivani. "That's what I wrote down."

"I feel like if I go through with this I will die and nobody will know about it. My body will keep moving but I'll be dead and nobody will know. Maybe it won't matter. Maybe that's the whole point."

"Why are we whispering," said Kalai. "Is it because the lights are off?"

"I was thinking of Damayanthi," whispered Aparna, furiously cracking her knuckles. "We spent the entire study holidays in final year together, the whole month. I don't understand how you can spend an entire month with someone and then that's it. Explain to me how that happens."

"Who's Damayanthi?" said Kalai.

"That American girl, she kept saying her name was Damn-My-Aunty, remember?" said Shivani. "She was from Idaho. Iowa. Something with 'I'."

Aparna opened her mouth in a silent sob; for a second she seemed suspended in time. Then Shivani tapped her on the shoulder.

"You have a pen I could borrow? Or a pencil?"

"What for?" said Aparna.

"I have to write this down."

"You're writing this down?"

"Or maybe you have a red colouring pencil? Or crayon?" said Shivani unfolding her chart.

"You're writing this down?" Aparna said again. She seemed to have said it louder this time and Kalai wondered if something was going to happen. She didn't feel prepared for anything violent and suddenly wished she hadn't come.

"How about a red felt pen?" said Aparna. "I have one that smells like cherries."

"Oh Damn-My-Aunty!" said Kalai, nodding her head. "Big, square girl. Looked like a box. Yes, I remember her now."

•

On the way home, Kalai looked down at her hands and began to miss them. She suddenly wondered if there were precautionary measures she should take, if there was some kind of compensation available somewhere.

"Aparna used to say 'bloody babies', remember?" said Shivani. "She never said 'bloody hell' or 'bloody fuck'. If it was something really mind-blowing she said 'bloodybastardbitch'. No babies."

"Bloodybastardbitchbabies."

"I actually thought she would become a banker. Somewhere in Coimbatore or Trichy maybe. I thought she'd have a room at the YWCA and she would go to church on Sunday. She would convert to Christianity and go to church, that's what I thought."

Shivani frowned and waved her forefinger in the air.

"I think I was mostly right, no?" she said. "What do you think?"

"I think that if it doesn't rain soon my hands are going to explode."

•

On their next visit, Kalai noticed that Aparna's house was in exactly the same state as they had left it. The American relatives were still sleeping with their socks on, the local relatives were still cutting vegetables and Aparna was still wearing the same clothes. Her room smelled sour and a laptop was glowing on the bed.

"I had Damayanthi's email," said Aparna. "She emailed back. And then I had to chat with her. I'm waiting for her to go to sleep. Isn't it night over there? Shouldn't she be sleeping now?"

"I think she just pinged you," said Shivani. "*Hey-babe-you-there.*"

Aparna slumped down on the floor and yawned.

"I actually saw this coming," said Shivani. "I wrote it down. In red, see?"

"She sent pictures of this trip she took to Vietnam," said Aparna. "Why would anyone go to Vietnam?"

"Or Germany," said Kalai. "I never got why people went to Germany."

"Take me out," said Aparna, getting up. "The two of you should take me out."

"Why?"

"Because I'm getting married. Buy me lunch or something. Take me to a movie. You have to take me someplace."

They waited in the corridor while Aparna got ready. Kalai sat on the floor and tried to flex her fingers.

"Why do we have to take her someplace? I don't want to take her someplace," said Kalai.

"We'll drive around and then she'll get bored," said Shivani, frowning at her chart. "I'm going to need another sheet of paper."

•

They hoped that Aparna would eventually ask them to take her home but she didn't. They ended up at Shivani's place, which was perched like an afterthought on a corner of somebody's roof. As soon as they arrived, Aparna sat down on the floor and took out a bottle of vodka and a notebook from her bag.

"So Kalai," said Aparna. "What do you say when people ask why you're still single?"

"I tell them my genitals fell off," said Kalai.

"How do you say genitals in Tamil?"

"I don't actually say genitals. I pat my upper thigh and say *ellaamai veezhinthiduchu.**"

"I hope you both have eaten something," said Shivani. "You guys can't be sick here, there's no water. I only get water in the morning and evening."

---

*   "They all fell."

64

"Do you know this old Tamil song?" said Aparna. *"Kaalam oru naal maarum / Nam kaavalaigal yaavum theerum / Varuvathu yennee sirikin-dren / Vanthathu yenne azhukindren.*"*

"No but have you ever noticed how old Tamil songs sometimes sound Chinese?" said Kalai. "I think it's all those twangy stringed instruments."

"How come there are no Tamil songs about genitals?" said Aparna. "How come I know the name for genitals in other languages but not in Tamil? Why is life fucked up like that?"

Shivani suddenly appeared holding a plate of fried eggs.

"What are you doing?" said Kalai.

"You don't eat eggs?"

"Why are you giving us eggs?"

"You have to eat something, I'm not having you two puking all over my house, there's no water."

"Kanavu kaanum vazhkaiyaavum / Kalainthu pohum kolangal," sang Aparna. *"Thuduppu kuda baaram endru / Karaiye thaidum odangal**."*

Aparna's song slowly disintegrated into a mess of sobs. She crumpled into a hiccoughing pile of broken girl, her elbows and knees flapping as if they were unsure of what to do.

"Don't cry," said Kalai, even though it seemed like a very useless thing to say.

"I want to know how this happened," sobbed Aparna. "How did all this happen?"

"Nothing happened," said Kalai.

"Exactly!"

"Nothing happens to a lot of people."

"Then what's the fucking point?"

Kalai became aware of her wrists, dangling beside her like broken tree branches. She couldn't feel her hands and for a second she wondered if they had fallen off.

---

* "The times will eventually change / Our troubles will come to an end / I laugh at what the future holds / I weep at what the past has held."
** "Every dream in life / Is just a design that will dissolve / Even when the oars become a burden / The boats start looking for the shore."

65

"How about a boiled egg?" said Shivani. "Or an omelet?"

•

Aparna sipped her vodka with a straw while Shivani dusted her bookshelf, swept the floor and rearranged her refrigerator. The plate of fried eggs hardened on the table and Kalai felt her hands grow heavier under the strain of the rainless sky and alcohol. She remembered a cartoon character whose hands kept changing into large hams and she thought, so that's what they mean. This is what they were trying to say. She began to bounce her hands on the ground, watching her fingers flail and curl like fat worms.

"I'm going to ask the landlady for extra buckets, evening water will be coming soon," said Shivani. "Make sure Aparna doesn't puke. If she does, make her puke in the garbage can."

"What if I puke?" asked Kalai.

"What did I just say, puke in the garbage can. I don't have a special place for your vomit."

Kalai slumped against the wall, overcome with mournful feelings and nausea. She saw herself laden with possibilities, each one hanging from her chest like a dead baby. Be proactive Kalai, she said to herself. Make a fist. Pray for rain. Wear a sari so the young men can see your waist. Carry your breasts like offerings. Don't fart in public.

Aparna suddenly lurched up, clutching her notebook.

"Have you ever felt like all you had left was the box?" she said. "Like you used everything else and then there was just the box?"

"What box?" said Kalai.

"Sometimes I think how we're born with these things—"

"Birth defects."

"No, we're born with things and they're like… ice sculptures. And it's like if we don't do something with the ice sculpture it melts and we are left with nothing. There's just the box. I mean if ice sculptures came in boxes, that's all that would be left. You know?"

"That's birth defects, what you're talking about. Sometimes they go away. I had a mole and I thought it would go away once."

Aparna stumbled across the room to the balcony, which had enough room for half a person to stand in. She climbed on the cement railing, swaying slightly.

"Kalai I'm so sorry your genitals fell off," said Aparna. "I don't know how you'll find a man now, considering you aren't very good-looking."

"What are you going to do?" said Kalai.

"Jump I guess. I can't think of anything else worth doing, can you?"

"Be proactive."

"This is proactive. It's something as opposed to nothing."

"Oh, then that's different. Then yes."

"Then you think I should do it?"

"Absolutely."

"You think I should jump off this balcony and kill myself."

"I really do."

Aparna nodded and climbed down again. She walked towards Kalai with huge, careful steps and then paused, as if she was thinking about something.

"You stupid, scummy fuck," she said.

"Hmm?"

Aparna suddenly began hammering her notebook into Kalai's ear.

"YOU STUPID SCUMMY FUCK," she shrieked. "Is that what you do? Is that what you say when someone is about to jump off a fucking balcony?

"Stop that!" yelled Kalai.

"You bloodybastardbitch! What the hell's wrong with you?"

"You're hitting my ear!"

"You stand there and tell me to jump? Is that what you do? You scummy dumbfuck!"

Kalai tried to cover her head with her hands but she couldn't feel them anymore. They've finally exploded she thought. It's finally going to rain.

•

Kalai was floating above twisty canals filled with vodka and ships. Her hands had become so huge that her fingernails were falling off, crashing into the canals and creating small tidal waves. The sailors whistled at her from below and said *hey baby, hey girliegirlie.*

"Thank you, you are too kind," Kalai called out. "Do any of you gentlemen know if it will rain soon?"

"Blow us a kiss and we'll tell you."

"Oh I couldn't possibly."

"Throw down your panties then."

"I can't get them off, my hands don't work."

"You're a waste of time," said the sailors, spitting into the canal. "We hope you get struck by lightning."

Kalai watched the ships disappear into tiny pink and orange sunsets. She thought it wouldn't be such a bad thing to be struck by lightning, to drown in twisty canals filled with vodka.

·

Kalai woke up on the floor with a pillow under her head. Shivani was sitting beside her, reading a magazine.

"Sleeping beauty!" said Shivani.

"She hit me in the ear, da," groaned Kalai, clutching her head.

"Hey guess what! I got four extra buckets of water today! You could even have a bath if you want! I mean, as long as you don't wash your hair. And not a long bath also."

"I can't hear anything, it's all ringy."

"Want to see a doctor? There's one just down the road, his name is Dr. Elvis Siluvairajan, does some kind of Muslim herb medicine or something. Which is strange I guess, considering his name is Elvis Siluvairajan."

"Where are my earrings?"

"I think they flew off when she hit you. Some were on the floor but I think you're missing a few."

"They're probably inside my ear. She kept hitting my ear."

"They're probably in your hair."

Kalai closed her eyes and tried to think of proactive things but she could only remember the sailors and how they spat into the canals.

"Did you write this down?" asked Kalai.

"Did I write what down?"

"That she kept hitting me in the ear like a crazy person? I think you should write that down."

"I can't remember where I put that paper, did you see it anywhere?" Shivani picked up a magazine, shook it out and frowned.

"Oh well," she said.

Kalai took a safety pin from her necklace, opened it and stabbed her thumb, feeling a wave of relief as the blood ballooned out like a tiny ruby.

The Butterfly Assassin

The Entomologist's smile is a tiny half moon, weak and incapable of casting any light.

"They will reconsider?" he asks.

"No, there's nothing they can do," says Malar. "You have to leave." Her mouth is sticky and sour from the heat but the Entomologist has only one bottle of water in his room. She wonders what will happen if she dehydrates and dies here.

"You told them who I was?" he asks.

"Yes."

"And what did they say?"

"They said there's nothing they can do. You have till Friday."

"Perhaps I should write them another letter."

"That won't help."

The Entomologist runs his fingers along the wall as if he is trying to find a secret door.

"Uncle, Friday means Friday. Okay?"

Malar watches as his hands crumple like dying spiders.

"Say okay."

The Entomologist nods but doesn't say anything.

·

Malar knows how to make killing jars. She has chronicled the life and death of the coconut beetle and arranged local butterflies in alphabetical order. She has paid the Entomologist's electric bills, swept his floor and made arrangements for his drinking water because she is a good person.

In the night she dreams that his room is carpeted with a thick green meadow. The sun glows in the corner, stabbing the grass in broad, fierce lines. Two large butterflies skirt the walls and the Entomologist chases them with a net and bottle.

"Don't clap your hands!" he says as he disappears under the sink. Malar looks down and sees millions of tiny butterflies burrowing into her palm, trying to fly from the tips of her fingers. She clenches her fists and feels the floor liquefy between her toes.

·

The next day Malar finds the Entomologist sitting on the floor with a pen and paper.

"I'm writing another letter," he says. "I don't think the other ones were strong enough."

Malar takes down his butterfly collection and arranges the boxes on the table.

"Why don't you wait?" says the Entomologist. "I think they might reconsider. This is a very strong letter."

Under his bed she finds newspapers bundled and stacked like building blocks. The Entomologist once said that words were sacred and should never be touched with the feet. Malar drags the bundles out to the head of the stairs. Then she kicks them down, one by one.

·

Malar is sitting on the grass in the Entomologist's room. She can hear the newspapers at the bottom of the stairs, wailing and cursing her with constipation and perennial bad breath. A large butterfly with shoe brushes on its feet hovers next to her, waiting for an explanation.

"Well it's not like I could carry them down by myself," Malar says. "It's not like he was going to help me."

Another butterfly with cobweb wings flutters above her head. The newspapers hope that Malar will get vaginal warts and grow a beard.

"Things are so much easier with a killing jar. It's quieter, you know," says the Cobweb Butterfly. "Have you ever been inside a killing jar?"

Malar rolls her eyes.

"I can't fit inside a killing jar, silly."

"Nobody can," says the butterfly.

·

The next day Malar brings a borrowed suitcase. The Entomologist has barricaded himself into a corner behind his butterfly collection.

"I'm not leaving," he says.

"Yes you are."

"What can they do? Will they throw me out in the street?"

"Yes."

"They can't do that. I'm an academician. I've been here for twenty years."

Malar begins piling his clothes into the suitcase. The scent of naphthalene settles on her tongue and she realizes that the Entomologist has always smelled like insect repellent.

"What about the butterflies?" she asks.

"I'm not going anywhere," says the Entomologist.

"You can take them in your hand or I can put them in the suitcase, there's still room."

"You're not listening to me."

"Or we can pack them tomorrow," she says. "I have to see the landlord about your key now anyway."

The landlord thinks that Malar is a saint and a blessing. Sometimes he makes his wife bring her ginger tea.

"Did you try speaking to the new owners?" asks the landlord.

"They said there's nothing they can do."

"That's a shame. It's a blessing you're here to help him at least. Else imagine! Where would he go?"

Malar thinks the Entomologist would probably sit in the street surrounded by his butterfly collection. He would sit there until someone ran him over.

"I'm not doing anything great," says Malar and the landlord shakes his head vigorously.

"No, no. You're a blessing. You're really a blessing. Have you managed to pack everything?"

"Everything except him," she says and they laugh. Malar feels her teeth flash like pieces of broken glass.

•

It is raining in the Entomologist's room and the clouds are bumping against Malar's forehead like bundles of wet cloth. The butterflies are under the sink, shaking the water from their wings.

"It's almost done you know," says Malar. "All I have to do is get him out of the room."

"You'll never do it without a killing jar," says the Cobweb Butterfly.

"I don't need a killing jar. Besides, he won't fit."

"It's not that hard," says the Shoe Brush Butterfly. "Everything in this world can fold, you know."

Malar doesn't think she will be able to fold the Entomologist that far. Even if she does she has a feeling he will break the bottle.

"I really don't think he will fit," she says.

"Nobody *fits* into a killing jar," says the Cobweb Butterfly. "They have to be *put*."

The rain begins to pound into Malar's skull like a shower of gravel. She wonders if she will catch a cold.

"Well good luck," says the Shoe Brush Butterfly. "Good luck from both of us."

The butterflies dip and soar into the thunderstorm like tiny slips of paper.

·

The Entomologist cuts a wobbly diagonal with his toes—sometimes an arc, sometimes a line. Sometimes he doesn't seem to be moving at all. Malar looks at his bloodied eyes and marvels that the ceiling fan didn't break.

Before hanging himself the Entomologist smashed every single one of his butterfly specimen boxes. Malar thinks he probably threw them on the floor, one by one. Or maybe he put his foot through them. She is not sure if he crushed the butterflies himself or whether they simply fell apart once the glass was broken. She finds a few specimen tags; Gossamer-Winged Butterfly, Brush-Footed Butterfly, Skipper Butterfly. She irons them out with her hand and places them on the table in alphabetical order.

Malar watches the Entomologist swing back and forth and tells herself that some people are like accidents. They are like sprained ankles and stains—they just happen.

"I am a saint and a blessing," Malar says and the words squirm inside her mouth like dying fish.

Jam That Bread of Life

Every morning I have breakfast with Annie. Annie doesn't like me but she insists we have our meals together because there is no one else here. All the normal people have gone home for the study holidays. The only ones left are the slackers and the poor students.

"Why are you still here?" I asked her one evening at tea. "You don't look poor to me."

"Why are *you* still here? Don't tell me you're planning on studying." She collapsed into a string of laughter that sounded like it was being hacked to pieces.

"Why would I do that?" I asked.

"That's what I meant. That's what I was trying to say."

Annie's laughter suddenly fell away and she sat staring at the table, her mouth angled awkwardly on her face.

This morning we're having bread—large, sticky loaves of sweet bakery bread with watery jam and silver cubes of butter. Above the food counter is a picture of Jesus Christ which is in a perennial state of almost falling over.

"Won't you get in trouble if you fail?" says Annie.

"Why are you so sure I'm going to fail?"

"Because you're not studying."

"What does that have to do with anything?"

Annie frowned and tapped the table thoughtfully.

"You should memorize quotes on success," she says. "They will keep you focused on your goals. Like this one: *They can because they think they can.*"

"They can what? Who are you talking about?"

"If you had a good quote, maybe you would take your studies a little more seriously."

"How about *Jam That Bread of Life*?"

"What?"

"It's on the bottom of that Jesus picture. See?"

"That says *I Am That Bread of Life.*"

"No it doesn't."

"Yes it does."

I pick apart the bread until I have a small, sticky mountain of crumbs. I think of giving this to the birds but there are no birds here. There are abnormally large red beetles that keep dying in the sun but no birds.

•

After breakfast, I start writing my Letter of Explanation to T.S. Eliot. I have already written one to Philip Larkin and I have made a paper tree for Samuel Beckett because I feel he would appreciate the tree more than the explanation. I have also written a note on the power of positive thinking for Sylvia Plath. I pull out a piece of yellow paper and a black fountain pen.

Dear Mr. Eliot,

I am writing to tell you that I am going to fail my paper on 20th century literature because I plan on answering all questions concerning The Waste Land *in a made-up language that will only consist of the letters y and p. I want you to know that it's not you, it's me. I'm sure you were a nice man, even though you worked in a bank. If I had known you, I promise I would have loved you.*

Annie doesn't call me for lunch and I forget about it completely until it is too late for lunch and too early for tea. I walk to Annie's room and open the door without knocking. She is sitting at her table, stabbing a pen into her desk as she mutters softly to herself. On the wall beside her is a poster that says *If you fail to plan, you plan to fail.*

"I think we missed lunch," I say.

"I had my lunch."

"Where was I?"

"I don't know."

"You didn't call me. Why didn't you call me?"

"I did call you. I mean I didn't know where you were."

The textbooks on Annie's study table are stacked in two piles. Between them lie a pen, a pencil and a bundle of scrap paper for Annie to practice writing out her answers. On her bed is a thin book called *Quotes for a Successful Life*.

"How's the studying going?" I ask.

She shakes her head, punctuating each shake with a stab to the table.

"But you've studied, right? You studied today?"

"Yes."

"You've been studying every day, haven't you?"

"Yes."

"So what's the problem? I don't understand."

She shrugs and continues to shake her head. Her stabbing has gouged a small hole in the table.

"You won't fail," I say. "How can you study like this and fail? I mean imagine studying as much as you have and then failing anyway. Just imagine that."

Annie stops shaking her head. After a few seconds, she stops stabbing the table.

•

I decide to make Annie a motivational poster. It will be on glossy black paper with bright orange handwriting and a picture of a German castle on a rock. Since I don't have a picture of a German castle on a rock, I make the poster using the back of an old receipt and a pencil.

"Knock!" says Annie when I enter her room. "Knock, knock, knock!"

"What?"

"Why can't you knock before you come in?"

"Here," I say thrusting the paper under her nose.

"What is this?" she says.

"It's to make sure you don't fail."

"Don't say that!"

"Stick it on your wall somewhere. Put it where you can see it."

"Jam That Bread of Lif," she says.

"What?"

"That's what you've written here, *Jam That Bread of Lif.*"

"Well, it will stop you from failing."

"Don't say that! Why do you keep saying that?" says Annie as I leave.

•

After tea, Annie starts throwing up. She keeps throwing up and has to be taken to the hospital. The warden says she will have to be put on drips because she has thrown up absolutely everything. There is nothing left inside her.

I have dinner alone and after that, I write a special Letter of Motivation and Explanation for Annie. I use white paper this time and a blue ballpoint pen. I bite the end of the pen and think. Then I walk to the window and think. I look at the moths slowly killing themselves against the porch light and I think. Then I sit down.

Dear Annie,

I hope that by the time you get this you will no longer be throwing up. My grandfather always said that throwing up was a good thing, along with diarrhea. It meant that the body was taking an active interest in clearing out things it didn't need. Tomorrow morning is your first exam and considering that you are probably on drips right now, you might be thinking that you won't be able to write your paper and you will fail and everyone will point fingers at you and you will kill yourself. This simply isn't true. I remember when I was in 9th standard there was a girl whose name was Thenmozhi and during our quarterly exams she had a bad case of dysentery which actually made her cry a little before the paper started. But she still wrote her exam and she still got the most marks. Now she has two kids and she is very fat.

The point is that you did not plan to fail. So even if you do, it's not really your fault.

Jam that bread of life. Always.

I fold the note into four and go to her room. I realize that like the other rooms in this corridor, Annie's room is empty but it's the only one that isn't locked. In fact, the door is slightly ajar, like the room is catching its breath. The white porch light has made everything look pale—the study table, the bed, the book of quotes. It's very still, except for a cricket that sounds like it's stuck somewhere under the bed. By tomorrow morning it will be dead and lying on its side. There must be something drastic, some life and death difference between the inside and outside that makes insects die like that.

I place Annie's letter inside her book of quotes, right between "Death" and "Dreams".

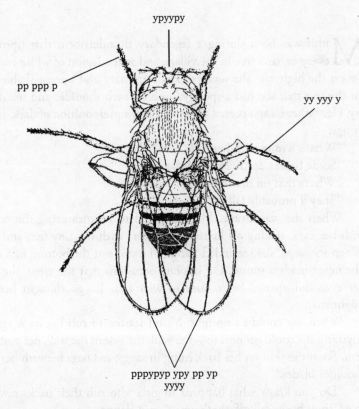

ypyypy

pp ppp p

yy yyy y

pppypyp ypy pp yp
yyyy

Fig. 5. A Literary Appreciation of T.S. Eliot's *The Waste Land*
Seen as a Diagram of a Mutant Fruit Fly.

FLYING AND FALLING

Muhil was born during a legendary thunderstorm that uprooted every banana tree in the village and sent a legion of white crabs to die on the highway. She was wrinkled, ordinary and unremarkable save for the fact that she had a spongy knob on each shoulder and she didn't cry. Her father Ilango peered at her and had a premonition of dark, heavy things.

"What's wrong with her?" he asked.

"Some babies don't cry," said the doctor.

"What's that on her shoulders?"

"They'll probably fall off."

When she was awake, Muhil seemed to be measuring the ceiling with her eyes, ticking off invisible numbers with her tiny fists and feet. When she slept, she reminded Ilango of a stone at the bottom of a river. She never made a sound. On the rare occasions that she cried, she shut her eyes and opened her mouth so wide that Ilango thought her jaw might snap.

When she could sit upright, Muhil started to rub her back against anything she could get next to—the wall, the side of the well, her mother's arm. Soon the skin on her back hung in saggy, red bags beneath her tiny shoulder blades.

"Do you know what happens to girls who rub their backs raw like that? Their backs fall off, that's what," said Ilango.

He took her to a doctor who peered at the folds of skin and tapped the knobs on her shoulder with a ballpoint pen.

"What's wrong with her?" asked Ilango.

"Nothing," said the doctor.

•

Soon people began to accost Ilango and his wife on the road and tell them stories of children that drank water from puddles and barked like wild dogs. These children had gone on to become doctors or lawyers in foreign countries. Surely Muhil would do the same. But a few months later, Muhil began to clamber onto small stools and throw herself to the ground. When stools were placed out of reach, Muhil began throwing herself off people's laps.

"Why are you doing this to me?" said Ilango. "No other child does this. I never did this to my father."

Muhil did not seem concerned. She kept tipping herself over any ledge she could find and Ilango stopped going out, because nobody could find anything heartening to say about children who seemed hell-bent on suicide so early in life.

•

A few nights later Ilango dreamed he was lying on the roof of his house, watching the afternoon sky. Even though the sun was out he could see clutches of green and orange stars blinking above him. He stretched out his hand and something circled down and landed on his palm. It was Muhil. Two tiny wings had sprouted from the knobs on her shoulders. They looked like dried leaves.

"So it's you!" said Ilango. "Those are very pretty wings you have."

Muhil looked up at him and bared her teeth; they were round and white.

"Why won't you talk to me," he asked. "Why won't you say anything?"

She stood up and began to walk across his palm, her wings rustling behind her like paper.

"Everyone thinks I'm a terrible father, because you keep trying to break your head open. I wish you would stop doing that."

Muhil teetered forward, the edges of her wings stabbing awkwardly at the sky. They reminded him of a dead tree.

"You will be the world's first flying doctor," mused Ilango. "Or flying lawyer. Or maybe you could do both. What do you think?"

Ilango watched as she tipped over the edge of his hand and spun out into the sky like a dying moth.

"That's all right," he said. "You can tell me later."

By the age of four, Muhil was crooked, stunted and more wrinkled than she was at birth. When she wasn't skinning her back against something she was tipping herself off anything she could climb. Her very existence had become uncomfortable to anyone who saw her. Well-meaning neighbors and friends began bringing pamphlets and newspaper clippings of places that kept children who couldn't be kept.

One evening Ilango sat with her on the back porch. Muhil kept pedaling against his arm, her breath coming in tiny, silent puffs as she tried to throw herself over the edge.

"Why?" said Ilango. "Why are you doing this? Look at your face. You know what people will think? They'll think I'm beating you up."

Muhil kept pedaling against his arm, her head lurching to the side as she tried to break free.

"Fine," said Ilango. "Go on. Break your head open."

He loosened his grip and Muhil pitched forward. Her tiny back curled and something shifted beneath her shoulders. Instead of falling, Muhil hovered in mid-air like a tiny hummingbird. Ilango saw the entire world swing from her shoulders as green and orange stars dripped from the sky. Then she crashed to the ground and split her lip open.

Ilango reeled under an overwhelming sense of understanding and purpose. Everything suddenly made sense and fit perfectly. He wondered how he hadn't seen it before. He arranged pillows around the wooden cot and held Muhil at the very edge.

"Try that again, what you did on the porch."

Muhil tipped over and landed face down in the pillows.

"Again," said Ilango. "Roll your shoulders, curl your back."

He tried the cot, the porch and the lower branches of the mango tree but nothing happened. He tried to catch her off guard, pushing her off the bed when she was napping but she still landed face down on the floor. He finally decided to take Muhil to the roof and his wife decided it was time to summon the police and all the neighbors. By the time Ilango was ready, a crowd of familiar heads and pointing fingers surged around his house.

"Ilango, put the girl down," called out his neighbor Pandian.

"Not yet."

"You're scaring her, Ilango, put her down."

"No."

"What? What did you say?"

"Not now, I need to try something."

Someone came from behind and grabbed Muhil from him. Ilango turned and saw her lurch against a tangle of arms, trying to throw herself over the edge.

•

Ilango spent the night in jail, staring at the floor. He held his hand out and thought, *this is how she floated. Roll your shoulders. Curl your back. This is how it's done.*

The next morning he came home to a house that was silent and empty. Pandian appeared at the door with a tumbler of coffee.

"Are they with you?" asked Ilango.

"They're fine," said Pandian. "What will you do for food? Shall I bring you something?"

"She isn't coming back?"

"Not right now."

Ilango watched the shadows spill across the walls and ceiling. He listened for the sound of a small body hitting the floor somewhere or the rustle of wings but he couldn't hear anything.

"We'll try again, that's all," said Ilango. "We'll just try again."

•

A week later Muhil and his wife were back home. Pandian came over in the evenings to make sure everything was all right. He also made half-hearted attempts at inspirational speeches.

"We've all made mistakes in the past," he said. "Important to look forward. Don't worry."

"Why should I be worried?" said Ilango.

"You need to be a good husband and father now. You need to remember that Muhil is sick."

"She's not sick. What makes you think she's sick?"

"You have to be responsible."

"Fine."

"I'm serious."

"So am I."

After supper Ilango would watch as Muhil clambered onto the cot and tipped herself onto a pile of pillows below. He felt a rustling in his brain telling him of flying doctors or flying lawyers or maybe both. Whichever she liked.

"We'll try again," said Ilango.

·

A few nights later Ilango took Muhil to an abandoned bridge at the outskirts of the village.

"Roll your shoulders, curl your back," he chanted as he carried her. "Say it with me, roll your shoulders, curl your back."

He turned her chin to the sky and made her look at the stars and the tops of the trees.

"You can go up there if you like. You can see nests and birds sleeping. Maybe you can see our house."

When they reached the bridge he held her on the edge of the railing and looked down. It was darker than he had thought it would be.

"Don't go far," he said as he slowly loosened his grip. "And come back quickly, do you understand?"

Muhil teetered for a second on the railing. Then she tipped sideways into the darkness like a bundle of old clothes.

Ilango stretched his hand into the darkness and waited.

Hoodoos

There are devastations inside Annamika's mouth, fluttering against her teeth like black butterflies. She tries to crush them with a jawbreaker.

"We're going to JasperAndBanff," says Andrea. "My Uncle Arby's got a cabin on Lake Louise. What's in Drumheller?"

"Dinosaurs," says Annamika. She doesn't like the word *hoodoos* so she doesn't mention them.

"I didn't know you were into dinosaurs."

"I'm not."

The jawbreaker rolls over Annamika's bottom lip and falls to the ground. Andrea doesn't give her another one.

•

The motel room has orange curtains that make it look like they are trapped inside a giant pumpkin. When the pizza comes, the delivery man smiles at her father and says "Salaam Aleikum."

"Why did he say that to you?" Annamika asks.

"Probably thought I was Muslim."

"Why would he think that?"

"The beard."

That night Annamika dreams of butterflies with beards. They line up outside the motel and demand to see the hoodoos. Her father brings them inside and points at the orange curtains. He points to Annamika and waves. The butterflies shake their wings and ask for their money back.

•

The hoodoos look like old men waiting for the bus. Annamika's father is wearing aviator sunglasses she has never seen before. He is suddenly unrecognizable.

"When are we going home?" she asks.

"We just got here. Don't you want to see the dinosaurs?"

"No."

"I thought you were into dinosaurs."

"I'm not."

Annamika watches her father point at the hoodoos. A hundred black butterflies beat against her teeth and step on her tongue. If she opens her mouth they will deflate the hoodoos like sandy balloons. They will cover the sky with their angry wings and her father will have nothing to point at.

THE QUEEN OF YESTERDAY

"**I** like to think of it as a talent. You know?"

Ruby gently wiggled her left nostril, as if she was about to sneeze. Then with a quick jerk, she tossed her head back.

"See?" she said. Two streams of blood were shyly inching from her nostrils. She let the blood trickle over her cracked lips and down her chin.

"Wow," I mumbled. Ruby grinned.

"I think there's something beautiful about bleeding noses, don't you?" she said, dabbing delicately at the streams of blood. "Not broken ones, just ones that bleed. Oh and lips that are cut at the corners—I *love* that, it looks so...gothic."

"Vampirish."

"Exactly."

"Starvedandbeatenartist-like."

"Yeah. Well no, maybe not that."

"You know, this might not be healthy," I said. Nosebleeds were delicately serious emergencies in my family. They were connected to something dark and traumatic that was lurking deep within a supposedly healthy body. Ruby glanced at me, carefully cradling the drops of blood in her hand.

"You're just jealous," she said quietly.

.

"FAKE nosebleeds, you mean." Jasmine was very insistent on this point. Making your body do something it wasn't supposed to was considered artificial in her world. She also didn't like Ruby very much.

"It was not fake, I saw the blood," I said.

87

"So she bleeds on request, big effing deal. I bleed once a month in a far more interesting place, you don't see me making a big deal about it. Did you know I could flip my eyelids?"

"What?"

"Want to see? I can flip them right now."

Jasmine began fiddling with her eyelids, twisting and turning them as she assured me she used to be really good at this.

A few minutes later we were on our way to the hospital.

•

While Jasmine shrieked beside me in the cab, I realized that our tolerance to pain changes over time. As children, a little pain isn't that big a deal. You climb a tree and scrape your knee. You put safety pins through your fingers. You get a nosebleed. This was the special power that Ruby still had. I could see it in the way she cradled the drops of blood in her palm, the way she shrugged off the disgusted stares.

"A lot of people think it's weird or gross," she said. "It's easy to think that, I guess. It's harder to think it might be something else."

"A good luck charm," I said.

"Sure."

"A rabbit's foot. A distinction with a bloody nose."

"Exactly. Not the rabbit one, the other one you said, the distinction one."

•

Jasmine's eyelid mishap was the result of manicured fingernails, contact lenses and toxic eyeliner all coming together at the wrong place at the wrong time.

"Will I ever see again?" she whispered as I took her home. Her head was sloppily wrapped in yards of thick white gauze with bits of cotton poking out of the sides. At my insistence, the nurse had put Tweety Bird stickers on the lumpy bandages covering her eyes.

"Three days. You'll be fine in three days; it's like a scratch on the skin, he said."

"Three days of darkness."

"You've never flipped your eyelids before have you?"

Jasmine sniffed silently.

"Have you?" I asked again.

"No."

.

As jealousy flitted behind Jasmine's Tweety Bird bandages, something extraordinary happened—Ruby tripped.

In a very unGothic turn of events, Ruby's fuzzy yellow banana slippers stalled during a routine dash down the stairs and remained on the third stair while Ruby went careening down and landed on her face. She did not just break her nose—she smooshed it. The blood ran onto the floor, slithering through her fingers as if it couldn't get away from her fast enough.

She opened her mouth to scream but ended up hiccoughing instead.

.

It was like watching your friend stare at the manhole that had just swallowed up their last quarter.

"Is it very bad?" I asked gently.

She blinked back tears and nodded.

"Ids breddy bad."

"Did you tell the doctor about—?"

She shook her head.

"I'm so sorry," I said, squeezing her hand.

As soon as her nose had healed, Ruby spent an entire afternoon trying to coax a little blood into her waiting palm. She twitched, tossed her head and then she asked me not to stare because it was distracting her. Nothing happened. She sneezed once but that was about it.

We no longer spoke of nosebleeds. It was something silly like trying to flip your eyelids. Now we spoke of important adult things that made us yawn and tap our coffee cups in a preoccupied way. Sometimes I would catch her out of the corner of my eye—she would gently turn her palms up, wiggle her nose slightly and I would hold my breath.

And nothing would happen.

The clock would start ticking again, a lawnmower would hum in the distance and I would pretend to be looking at something else.

Ruby would sigh, crumple up her hands and ask for another cup of coffee.

MURALI

Murali is tapping his fingers to his forehead, trying to remember something. His shoulders are hunched over and his feet twitch sporadically.

"What? What is it?" I ask.

He sighs and shakes his head. I trace the letter 'S' down his back and yawn. When I open my eyes, Murali is gone. I look under the bed and behind the chair. I call out his name but no one answers.

•

"Diya?"

"What? What happened?"

"He's gone."

"Who?"

"Murali."

"What do you mean he's gone?"

"I mean he was sitting right beside me and I yawned and now he's gone."

"Don't be silly, he probably left."

"He couldn't have left, he doesn't know how to open the door. Meaning it sticks and he can't get it open by himself."

"Is this some kind of joke? Do you two have me on speaker phone or something?"

"No, he's really gone."

"Listen, call me back."

•

I begin to tabulate everything I know about him. He is left-handed and has scars on his feet from a bike accident. He collects butterfly wings and hides them between the pages of an empty pocket diary. He never wears a watch. He believes that my door is haunted. Sometimes he thinks there are tiny demon-hands holding it shut. Sometimes he just kicks it and says "Stupid fuck."

"How come *I* can get it open?" I asked him once.

"Because you're haunted too," he said.

I open the window to see if he has fallen out and broken his ankle but he isn't there.

.

"It's Diya. Is he back yet?"

"No."

"Are you high or something? It's okay if you are but are you sure he was there?"

"I'm sure. I don't know. I thought he was here."

"Okay. That's okay."

"Diya, I need you to come let me out."

"What do you mean?"

"I can't get the door open, it's stuck."

"Okay. Okay hold on."

.

The light dims and bends on the floor like liquid. Murali suddenly seems to be everywhere at once, in coloured bits and pieces. I remember the curve of his teeth, how I sometimes felt like shrugging him off like a heavy overcoat. I think of all the questions people will ask.

Were you the last person with him?

Yes.

How often do you lose things in your room? Have you ever lost a person before? How well did you know him?

I know that he hummed when he peed. I know that as a child, he thought girls came from their mothers and boys came from their fathers.

Was anything bothering him?

He didn't like my door. He thought it was vindictive and haunted.

Did you make him disappear?

I don't know.

"Hey, it's me Diya. I'm knocking, can you hear me knocking?"

"Yes."

"Ok, so how do you want to do this?"

"Pull the door towards you when I say."

"Ok. Now?"

"No wait. Okay now try."

"Fuck. What happened?"

"I don't know. Usually I can open it fine. I don't know what happened today."

"Is he still gone?"

"He's not here. I don't know what happened."

"Everything will be okay. I'm going to get somebody to help open the door and then we're going to figure this out. We'll go look for him, how about that? I'm sure he'll be there."

"Where?"

"We'll find him, don't worry. We'll figure this out."

•

I picture roots shooting out like sprays of black lightning, anchoring the door into places filled with broken things. I don't think they'll be able to get the door open. I don't think anybody will be able to do anything.

The evening fades into a thick, dark smudge, swallowing the lines and corners of my room. The only thing I can see is my pillow which is lying on the floor. There is no trace of Murali—no fingerprints, no butterfly wings, no notes saying "gone fishing" or just "gone". It is like he was never here.

I sit beside the door and listen as a forest of broken bones blossoms inside me.

A Bottle of Wings and Other Things

The spider was balled up like a tiny, brown fist in a dusty corner of Ganesan Brothers Private Limited Company. There was no extravagance in its death; just a gentle curl, a folding which no one had seen or heard. Alarmel got up from her table and went to have a better look. The spider's husk seemed skittish, as if life had weighed it down and it was now ready to tumble away to bigger and brighter things. She pulled out a small notebook and wrote:

> *Who will brave us when they save us?*
> *We have the beauty of the flowers in case everything else sours.*
> *The cockroach would surely sing if it was made of other things.*

At the end of the day, she wrapped the spider in a piece of paper and took it home with her. She decided that she would eventually bury it or place it on her windowsill. Or maybe she wouldn't do anything at all. For the time being, she put it inside an old Horlicks bottle and looked at it under her table lamp. At first it reminded her of a flower that had closed and had no intention of opening again. Then it reminded her of a lamp that she had seen in a craft store. She pulled out her notebook and wrote:

> *A sneeze like a spider all tied up inside her.*
> *Love is like a butterfly that turns and tumbles in the sky.*

For a split second, Alarmel wondered if she was a poet. She thought she probably wasn't since none of what she had written made any sense. Maybe I'm a senseless poet, she thought to herself. She looked at the bottle and heard something blossom at the bottom of her heart.

•

During the next few days, Alarmel scoured the office and found two moths, a bee and a handful of caterpillars that seemed to have died in a cluster. She added them to the bottle and wrote:

In the room the women come and go, don't ask them why 'cause they
*   don't know.*
My love is like a redred rose that's drowned beneath the garden hose.
Things out of season in a garden become like reason and start to harden.
What is this life if full of care we have nothing to eat or wear.

The bottle no longer seemed like a bottle; in fact, Alarmel thought it looked more like a bubble filled with legs and broken chest cavities. She felt less inclined to bury it now. It seemed like an entirely new entity that had grown out of shards of exoskeleton and bent phrases.

One morning, when there had been very little in the way of dead insects, the man who sat at the next table suddenly jumped up, his arms flying out like he was holding the world back from some large and imminent danger.

"Look," he said, pointing into the binding of an accounts ledger. Nestled inside was the carcass of a large, fat silverfish, almost the size of Alarmel's thumb.

"It's just a silverfish, Velu," said Alarmel, as she carefully slid her pencil tip under it and scooped it up.

"I've never seen one so big, have you?" said Velu. "I thought it was a lizard, dirty bugger. Just toss it out the window."

"Yes, alright," said Alarmel as she folded it carefully into a piece of paper. That evening she dropped the silverfish into the bottle where it promptly crumbled to pieces. She wrote:

A silverfish in a silver dish.
Behold the long and short of it—sometimes jasmines smell like shit.

•

Velu always came to work breathless and disoriented with beads of sweat dripping down his nose and forehead. It would take ten minutes and an entire bottle of water for him to find his bearings and Alarmel often wondered if he ran all the way to work. The next morning, after sweating profusely under the fan and downing his morning bottle of water, Velu turned to her.

"So you threw that silverfish out?"

"I took it home."

"For what? You keep fighter fish?"

"Yes," lied Alarmel.

"I heard they eat mosquitoes."

"They eat anything."

"Really? You mean like rice?"

"No, insects. He eats anything that's dead."

The next day, Velu brought her a large, green dragonfly with a string attached to its tail.

"I was flying this last evening," said Velu. "I used to fly them all the time when I was a boy. We would all go to the river and catch them by the tail and then fly them on the way to school. Will he eat it?"

"Who?"

"Your fighter fish."

"Oh yes," said Alarmel, folding the dragonfly into a piece of paper. "He'll eat anything."

•

Every morning Velu brought her something different—a large black spider, a broken rainbow beetle, a butterfly with a torn wing. Velu would place them on her table like flowers and tell her how he was bitten by a scorpion when he was a boy, how his uncle had died of snakebite. Alarmel would fold each insect into a piece of paper and write things like:

For now the way is very clear for measuring the atmosphere.
Shells and ships travel in clips and crash against our fingertips.

The bottle was now a clogged and crumbly mess of bodies, some of which had completely turned to dust. Alarmel bought a sheet of white foolscap paper and copied down everything she had written so far in her notebook. Instead of listing the phrases, she let them run into each other like an unending train of words. When she was finished, she read it back and realized it made absolutely no sense. Sometimes it was awkward, sometimes it was just plain silly.

But on the whole, it was the most perfect thing she had ever read in her entire life.

•

The next morning, after Velu had given her a handful of ladybugs, Alarmel handed him the piece of foolscap paper, neatly folded into a white square.

"What's this?" he asked.

"Just read it and tell me what you think."

"Is it your resumé? Are you looking for another job?"

"Nothing like that, just read it."

Alarmel waited for him to read it during the day, then reminded him about it before he went home. The next morning, Alarmel came in early and waited. People came in and looked at her with a smile and raised eyebrows—"You've come early!" they said and she nodded and said yes, I came early. As usual, Velu arrived drenched in sweat, his eyes popping out of his face. He drank deeply from his water bottle then came to her table and pulled up a chair.

"I'm so sorry," he said and began wiping his face.

"Why, what happened?"

"See my friend Prabhu had to book train tickets—his parents are going to Tirupati. Have you been there?"

"No."

"I haven't either. Not recently anyway, got my first head-shaving done there, when I was little. Anyway he needed to write down their names because they changed the spelling recently, numerology you know. You believe in numerology?"

"No."

"I don't either. Anyway he took that paper to write on and never returned it. He didn't return my pen either. It was a nice one, gel tip. I am very sorry, I hope it wasn't important."

Alarmel said it wasn't and Velu placed three coconut beetles on her table and left. Alarmel began to feel things shift inside her head. The more she thought about it, the more she realized that the dead insects in the bottle were just dead insects in the bottle. By lunch time, Alarmel decided that if she pulled out her notebook again, it would be to make shopping lists. She wouldn't even look at dead insects. She would become a productive person, join a computer course and walk briskly for thirty minutes every day, breathing deeply with full lung capacity. She would do embroidery in her free time and go to the temple every morning. Most importantly, she would bury the insect jar the minute she got home. That evening, Alarmel sat in front of the bottle, hands folded, writing absolutely nothing. Before going to bed, she told herself that she would bury the bottle tomorrow.

The next day, Velu arrived with a noolpuzha honeybee. It was curled in the palm of his hand, like it was asleep.

"Very small, no?" said Velu. "I thought it was a fly and hit it with a newspaper. He eats bees?"

"Who?

"Your fighter fish."

"He's dead."

"Why? What happened?"

"I don't know. I came home and he wasn't there. I mean he was dead."

"He probably jumped out of his tank."

"Yes."

"Sometimes they do that. Don't worry, you lose something, you find something."

Alarmel watched Velu walk back to his table and thought:

When I die, don't bury me, just throw me in the sky and see if I can fly.

She opened her notebook and made a strict note to herself not to write any of that down.

•

Against her better judgment, Alarmel took the honeybee home. She placed it in front of the bottle and thought:

A poet is like a jar that has gone too far.
Honeybees are full of fleas.

She gently pulled the honeybee's wings off and placed it on the end of her finger. For some reason it reminded her of a kitten.

Smitten with stinging yellow kittens.

No, no, Alarmel said to herself. Computer courses. Pray with furrowed brow and promise God that you will walk briskly and breathe with complete lung capacity. Above all, make it a point to make sense.

The tiny bee seemed to be edging along her finger and Alarmel thought she heard a rustling coming from the jar. It seemed like all the wings and legs and abdomens were shuffling together while the bottle swelled like a transparent balloon. Alarmel closed her eyes and saw words slipping across the back of her eyelids:

What is it about the sun that makes it burn for everyone?
Beneath the yawning velvet bee the village smithy broke his knee.
Crumbly is as crumbly does to forget about what crumbly was.

Take computer courses with full lung capacity, Alarmel murmured to herself. Pray to everything that walks briskly and sensibly.

Alarmel opened her eyes and saw that the bottle was neither rustling nor swelling. The bee however, had disappeared. Alarmel looked for it on the floor, inside her clothes and then inside the bottle in case she had dropped it in without thinking. After an hour, she was forced to come to the conclusion that she must have inadvertently eaten it.

·

The next day, Alarmel spoke to a colleague about computer classes, noting down course structures and module formats that cluttered up her notebook like a cloud of gnats. Whenever she found herself thinking of insects, she pulled out a piece of paper and did long division. Velu came at lunch and patted her table reassuringly.

"You lose something, you find something, no?" he said.

"I didn't lose anything."

"Your fish died—isn't that a loss?"

"Oh yes. Yes it is."

He reached into his pocket and pulled out a folded piece of paper that looked like it had been washed.

"And see what I found? I said Prabhu forget the pen, I can buy a new pen. But you better find that paper. I mean it wasn't even mine—what if it was important? What if it was a will?"

"It wasn't a will."

"Anyway, it got washed but I could still read it. He said to say he was sorry."

Velu smoothed the paper out on the table and pulled up a chair.

"So what is this exactly?" he asked.

"What do you mean?"

"I didn't think it was a story because there are no people. Unless this is a story without people. Is it?"

"I don't think so."

"So it's a poem."

"I don't know. It's words."

"*Behold the long and short of it—sometimes jasmines smell like shit.*"

"I didn't mean to say shit."

"That's jaathimalli of course. Dirty bugger of a flower. I always thought it smelled like a toilet. *What is this life if full of care we have nothing to eat or wear?* I like that one a lot."

"Really?"

"Yes, it's about poverty, isn't it? Because if life is full of care and there is nothing to eat and wear then that must mean you're poor of course."

"Of course."

Velu folded the paper up again and put it in his pocket.

"I think it is important to discuss things like this," he said. "Expands the mind. My father always made me read English newspapers when I was a child. And see? Now I'm able to discuss poetry with you. Tell me when you write something else."

Velu walked back to his table and sat down. Alarmel watched as he bent over a file, his back curving away from his chair. She thought of the honeybee he had brought her, how it had looked like it was sleeping in the palm of his hand.

Rebellion, often instigated by real or
perceived inspiration, resulting in a belief
that something can be created that the
world has never seen.

Reassurance that the creation is not only
completely original, it will also cure cancer
and make everyone love you.

Realization that the new creation bears a
striking resemblance to an old creation.
This is often coupled with a simultaneous
unwillingness to let go of the old creation.

Resolution, after finally letting go,
to try again.

Fig. 6. Various Stages in the Development of the Artist
Represented by the Emergence of a Dragonfly

The Goddess of Dislocation

By Sunday evening, we were in trouble. We knew we were going to be in trouble for some time now. At one point, Kayalvizhi had even stood up and stamped her foot.

"Machan, what are we doing, da?" she said. "We're sitting here plucking pubic hairs*, that's what we're doing. We're fucking useless."

I agreed because there was nothing else I could do. I pointed out that we were also taking up space, wasting time and going bad and Kayalvizhi nodded because it was all true. Now it was Sunday evening and here we were, sitting on the floor, so fucking useless. We had just eaten what was left of the food, which was cold rice and ketchup. Thankfully that was the last of it, so even though we were in trouble, at least we didn't have to eat cold rice and ketchup anymore.

---

* I feel compelled to say a few words about the phrase "plucking pubic hairs", which is a rough translation of the Tamil phrase *mayir pudingrathu*. The word *mayir* means hair and in certain places I've heard it used in an ordinary sense—*mayir alavu*, for example, is used to say "a hair's breadth". But in other areas, particularly in the city, *mayir* means pubic hair. So *mayir pudingrathu* usually means "plucking pubic hairs"—it's not something nice people are supposed to say. I want to mention that I believe that the meaning may differ, depending on how people use it. In my limited scope of experience, the phrase is meant to imply that state of being where someone is so jobless or useless that they were actually spending their time pulling out their pubic hairs one by one. Some people drop the *mayir* completely and just say *pudingrathu*. Sometimes the term *pudingi* is used, which means "a person who plucks". Physical gestures are also commonly used. Generally, people pretend to be plucking the hair on their head or arm, though I've seen the more risqué mimic the act of plucking the hair on their upper thighs. I've also seen the phrase translated into English, as literally and shoddily as possible, like "Bloody plucker why you are sitting and simply plucking?"

Also, due to a strange quirk of the Tamil accent, the English *p* and *f* sounds are often interchanged, the result being that "plucker" becomes "flucker", which is one of those great words which sounds like fucker but isn't because it's flucker.

Anyway, that's all I have to say about that.

"Look at us," said Kayalvizhi, "Why are we just sitting here? We should *do* something!"

"I know," I said and felt a sob quiver at the back of my mouth. I put my head down and hoped I would be sick. I felt that everything would be alright if I got sick.

"I mean we're lucky we're even here," said Kayalvizhi. "Imagine if Asha hadn't let us crash here when she left. Then where would we be?"

"We'd be dead," I said, trying not to bawl.

"Worse. We'd be sitting in a ladies hostel in Guduvancherry."

"We'd be wearing nighties all day. We'd be drying our underwear on buckets hidden under our beds."

"We have to do something. Maybe we should do something with the computer."

I got up and made my way to the bathroom. By the time I reached the toilet I was sick; not halfway sick like spitting up bile and belching but real, throw-it-out-start-again sick. I flushed the toilet and put my head under the tap. I was sure that now, things could only get better.

.

Kayalvizhi mailed Asha to tell her we were in trouble, though she didn't say what the trouble was. After all, it wasn't anything specific—it was all sorts of trouble snarled up together. Asha mailed back the next morning, assuring us that we could do anything in the whole world because we could write in English. I recited the alphabet to see if it made me feel empowered but I got lost somewhere between L and R.

"So apparently there's this person looking for articles," said Kayalvizhi.

"Articles of what?" I asked.

"India. Food articles. Temple articles. Sari articles. Asha said they'll pay two hundred dollars. That's about eight grand. Four for you, four for me."

"We could get... all sorts of stuff."

"Yes we could."

"That would take care of everything. No more trouble."

"Exactly. So I was thinking we could do temples."

"Oh definitely. There's one on the corner, let's do that one."

"Not big ones."

"This one isn't big, it's more like a shrine really. You can't see it if a cow stands in front of it."

"I mean let's do something like village temples. Something that's got a lot of rice fields around it."

"Well, there's this temple down by Nagercoil that's got two goddesses instead of one."

"Is it in a rice field?"

"Probably. The thing is that the goddesses are sisters, one's the bad goddess and the other one's the good goddess. Or something."

"Or maybe we should do abandoned temples. Haunted temples."

"I think the younger one is bad. Or maybe it's the other one. Maybe they're both bad. Or no, they can't be bad, can they? I don't think goddesses can be bad."

"Haunted houses! Oh, let's do haunted houses!"

I looked down at my hands, thinking about the sister goddesses, one good and one bad. Maybe that's how we were built intrinsically—one bad eye, one good eye. One bad elbow, one good elbow. And all those yinyang body parts worked together to make a complete person.

"I just had an amazing thought," I said but by the time I had Kayalvizhi's attention I had forgotten what I wanted to say.

•

We decided to go with the sister goddesses because Kayalvizhi thought a bad goddess was almost like a haunted house. We Skyped Asha, to let her know what we were doing.

"Oooh that's nice," said Asha. "I like that. Is it like a Dalit thing?"

"A what?" said Kayalvizhi.

"You know, lower caste goddess thing. You guys aren't Dalits, are you? Because I didn't mean it in a bad way."

"No, I don't think we are."

"Fabulous. Then you both should go down to Madurai—"

"Nagercoil."

"Right, go to Nagercoil and check the place out."

"But we already know it's there."

"Right, but you have to go there to get more information."

"Why? It's a temple with two goddesses and they might be sisters, what more do we need to know?"

"Interview a Tamil history professor or something, give it some brains. Talk to old people. Lots and lots of old people."

"Old people don't like us."

"And try and get pics of the old women with the big ear holes, you know what I mean? The ones that have those huge piercings that you could fit your arm through? And send me a mail once you get to Madurai, okay?"

Asha hung up and I thought I was going to be sick. I would much rather be in trouble than in a train or a bus, traveling with large-elbowed women who kept asking if I was married.

"I can't do it," I whispered, putting my head down. "I give up."

"Wait, I know why she thought we should go there," said Kayalvizhi. "I know why she said that. She doesn't know that it's fourteen bloody hours to Nagercoil. By bus. And we can't travel in a bus for fourteen hours. You'd get sick, for one thing."

"I could get sick just thinking about it."

"So we're going to ignore what she said on account of the reality of our circumstances. I mean she's obviously out of touch with everything here, she's been gone for like... a month?"

"Three days."

"Anyway, I think we can do pretty well from here. Chennai is the city and the city is everywhere, right?"

"Right."

"And we can take pictures of pictures. I think we can do that."

"Right. And we can do that from here too. We don't have to go anywhere."

•

Kayalvizhi found an abandoned notebook and we sat down to work seriously on the article. For the first few minutes we were stunned by how much we were going to achieve. We were on the brink. We were almost superstars.

"So, sister goddesses," said Kayalvizhi.

"Right, so they're sisters but I'm wondering if they're goddesses. I mean what if they were just magic or something?"

"Magic sisters."

"That used to happen, you know. People turning magic and moving statues with their minds and stuff. Walking on water. Maybe it was like that."

"Did they build temples for magic people back then?"

"I'm pretty sure they did."

Kayalvizhi put her book down and frowned at the floor.

"I think that happens to me sometimes," she said.

"What?"

"Well I don't think I should talk about it directly because it might lose its power. But I get what you're saying about magic people."

"What am I saying?"

"How people can do magic. I'm not saying that about me though, because it might lose its power."

"You're telling me you're magic."

"Not directly. Directly I'm not saying anything."

"Do something then. Make your hand disappear."

"It doesn't work that way."

"How does it work then?"

"It's very quiet. It's like… knowing… only in a very quiet way."

"Knowing what?"

"I don't think you'd get it if I told you."

"Fine. I feel pukey anyway."

"Ok. We'll do this later."

Kayalvizhi spent the rest of the day in the next room and all I could see of her was her foot, dangling over the edge of a chair. Sometimes it moved like it was happy and dancing for a very special reason. Sometimes it just hung there and I wondered if she had died.

•

The next day we barely spoke, not even when we noticed a small rat scuttling across the floor of the kitchen. I found a packet of Tang and poured half of it into a bowl, leaving the other half for her on the counter. In the afternoon I fell asleep and dreamed that I was chasing Kayalvizhi down a deserted street, asking her to make her hand disappear. She ran to an intersection and suddenly split in two, one half running to the right, one half to the left. I stood at the junction, unsure of which one to follow. When I woke up, I found that I had spilled Tang all over my arm and onto my bed. Kayalvizhi was sitting on the ground, sorting through old newspapers.

"What are you doing?" I asked.

"Looking for old Sudoku games. You like Sudoku? I *love* Sudoku."

"Did you write anything yet?"

"No, did you?"

I shook my head and began dusting the Tang off my arm.

"You know what it is?" said Kayalvizhi. "We're just sad and tired. That's what's wrong with us."

"And sick."

"I think we need some inspiration. We should tell Asha's landlady that we have the flu."

"Tell her we're getting viral fever."

"Right. We have the flu and viral fever and if we don't do something about it soon, we'll…we'll what?"

"We'll melt."

"Right, something like that."

Kayalvizhi quickly changed her clothes, washed her face and tied her hair up.

"Shouldn't you comb it?" I asked.

"I'm afraid," she whispered.

"Of what?"

"I'm afraid there's something living in my hair and it will fall out if I comb it. I haven't combed my hair all week."

"You mean like lice?"

"No," she said, shaking her head. "Something far worse."

I watched her leave and wondered what could be living in her hair. Whatever it was, I had a feeling it was living in my hair too.

•

Kayalvizhi was gone long enough for the sky to turn dark and the mosquitoes to emerge from the gutter to start their symphony. I hummed along with them, harmonizing from the other side of the window. Kayalvizhi returned with a wire basket filled with food.

"She wanted us to come over for dinner but I said you were too sick," said Kayalvizhi. "We can come for breakfast tomorrow if we're up to it."

"And?"

Kayalvizhi pulled out two strips of tablets from her pocket.

"Paracetamol," she said. "Better than nothing I thought."

We put the wire basket in the refrigerator and pulled out two bottles of water, one each. We held our strips of paracetamol up to the light, then tapped them on the side—Kayalvizhi said this made the dust settle but I did it for good luck. Then Kayalvizhi stretched out on a mat on the floor while I lay down on the sofa.

"Remember to be inspired," she said. "Think sister goddesses. Think Nagercoil. Think haunted houses."

"Not haunted houses. We're doing temples."

"Ok so think temples. Temples temples temples."

It was a long wait. I watched lights blink on in the apartments outside and wondered what the people up there were doing, what they were eating, if they ever looked out the window and wondered about us. I turned and looked at Kayalvizhi, who was frowning at her fingernails.

"Kayal," I hissed.

"Hmm?"

"Do some magic."

"No."

"Come on, pull your head off or something."

"Temples, machan. Temples Temples Temples."

"Right."

I closed my eyes and found myself thinking about bones instead of temples. It occurred to me that if approached in the correct manner, the world could be peeled and on the inside there would be plastic bags and hair but mostly bones. Temples Temples Temples, I thought but all I could see were clean, white bones, overlapping and knocking together like dead branches. I opened my eyes and glared at the ceiling, frustrated with my brain, frustrated with the paracetamol. I turned to look at Kayalvizhi.

She was sitting up and yawning. Two sets of arms were gently opening like wings from her back.

"What happened?" I asked.

"Don't worry about it, we don't have to go anywhere. We're the goddesses," said Kayalvizhi. She sat straight and smiled as her six arms opened out like lotus petals. As an afterthought, she raised one hand in blessing.

"Well?" she said.

"Can you do the tongue thing?" I asked.

Kayalvizhi frowned, then suddenly held her tongue out as her eyes flared wide open.

"Doesn't really fit for some reason," I said.

"Thought not. I don't feel like I should be doing the tongue thing."

She got up and began pacing the room with a slight spring in her step. I shrugged my shoulders to see if extra arms would fold out but nothing happened.

"It's us? You're sure?" I asked.

"Yes. I mean just look at these arms."

"So who's the good one?"

"Oh I don't know. We can both be the good one."

"How come I don't have any extra arms?"

"Maybe they're growing. Or maybe you're supposed to do the tongue thing."

She began humming an old Hindi tune, kicking her feet out, jumping to the left, then the right. One set of her arms hung limply at her side, like they didn't want to be a part of anything that was happening. I looked down at my hands, listening for some sort of magic that might be humming at my fingertips.

"*Mera naam Chin Chin Choo*," sang Kayalvizhi.

"*Chin Chin Choo Baba Chin Chin Choo*," I mumbled.

"*Raat chandini mein aur tu, Hello Mister how do you do?*"

Kayalvizhi began spinning faster, stamping the ground with her feet. "Second verse, same as the first!" she shouted, her arms whipping above her head. A premonition of bad things was slowly soaking into me. If we were goddesses then we were supposed to be quiet and wise. We were supposed make sure that the sun rose and people who were sexually immoral got genital warts.

"Stop it Kayal," I said.

"What?"

"Stop it, you'll break something."

"How?"

"A goddess isn't supposed to move so quickly. It'll make black holes or something."

Mera naam Chin Chin Choo.

"You're going to make children get born with horses' heads. Everyone's knees will disappear."

Chin Chin Choo Baba Chin Chin Choo.

The room felt like it was being stretched like a rubber band, just waiting to split. I closed my eyes and saw splotches of dirty orange seeping into the frozen silhouette of Kayalvizhi's spinning body.

"Fuck," said Kayalvizhi.

I opened my eyes and saw her standing in front of me, shaking her head. Blood was running from my lips and down my chin in thick rivulets.

"Is this cancer or something? Is the world bleeding?" I asked.

"Did you try the tongue thing?" asked Kayalvizhi.

I shook my head, holding my hands over my mouth. Kayalvizhi wandered to the other side of the room, singing under her breath *Mera naam Chin Chin Choo, Chin Chin Choo Baba Chin Chin Choo.*

•

When I woke up the sun was in my face and the sound of a drill was hammering away somewhere in the distance. Kayalvizhi was standing beside the sofa, frowning down at me.

"You puked all over yourself," she said.

A sticky chain of vomit trailed across my face and into my hair. I put my hands over my eyes, trying to block out the sun.

"All you had was the paracetamol? You're sure?" said Kayalvizhi.

I nodded. Kayalvizhi shrugged and sat on the floor.

"That's funny. You've never done that on paracetamol before. Don't you think that's funny?"

I wanted to shake my head but I ended up nodding again.

"Asha mailed," she said. "We missed the deadline for the sister goddesses thing so she wrote something herself about some temple at her grandmother's place. Which I think is a bit like stealing because that was what we were going to do. Haunted temples, remember?"

My body felt heavy and sour like a rotten lime. I realized that I couldn't feel my tongue and wondered if I had swallowed it.

"We better figure out something else or we're going to be in trouble," said Kayalvizhi, stretching out on the mat. "There has to be something we can do."

I tried to think of things we had done, things we were capable of doing. I wondered if I should try and be sick again but I had a feeling I would only cough up lost children and bags filled with dead kittens.

I closed my eyes and watched as the sun slowly ground its heels into my eyelids.

Miraculous

Every Sunday afternoon my roommate ascends the crumbly stairs to our rooms, her overnight bag filled with misgivings, dirty underwear and papayas. The misgivings are for what she has done over the weekend. The papayas are for dissolving her eggs.

"Why don't you just use a condom?" I ask as she hacks the fruit into large uneven pieces that will not fit into her mouth.

"We didn't have one."

Hack hack.

"We never have one."

Sunday afternoons remind her that before there was Population Control and social workers with bulging bags of contraceptives, there was the papaya. If she eats too many she ends up with a bad stomach or heat boils. Sometimes she ends up with both.

•

James the Office Genius is a man with no earlobes and long, pale fingers like church candles. He wears an army vest with four pockets because he doesn't use the pockets in his pants.

"A mouse?" I ask.

"Yes. You want to see it?"

"Does it have two heads?"

"No."

"Then I don't want to see it."

James takes the mouse out anyway.

"Found it a week ago on my way home. Totally dead but it hasn't decayed or anything. Cool, nah? Named him Miraculous."

James gently touches its tiny pink nose before putting it back in his pocket.

"I don't get it," I say, "How come you never use the pockets in your pants?"

•

Once upon a time on a Sunday my roommate moved in with three black suitcases. She lined her cupboards with newspaper and arranged her clothes in uneven piles, strewing naphthalene pellets around them to keep the bugs away. She had a bowl of cut papaya beside her which she periodically dipped into.

"Best fruit. Clears your skin, pumps you up with vitamins. This is a good one, sweet. You want?" she said.

"No, I don't like the smell," I said.

"You just take if you want. So what do you do again?"

"Nothing much."

"You're working right?"

"Right."

"Me too. So is it like tight work or you get like some time for yourself?"

"Yes."

"Cool. I probably won't be here on the weekends, that's when I meet my boyfriend, only time we're both free. What you do on the weekends?"

"Nothing... much."

"Oh hey there's some extra papaya in the kitchen also, you can have if you want. Or just take from here, there's lots."

By the time she settled in, it was clear that she was the Queen of Papayas and I was the Queen of NothingMuch.

•

One day Miraculous the Mouse falls under the table and lands beside a five rupee coin. The five rupee coin buys James one watery tea and one samosa which contains an oily cockroach. The tea stall owner apologizes and offers to give James a free tea and samosa every day if he promises not to tell anyone.

"Miraculous," says James as he shoves the mouse into my palm. I hold it too tightly, feeling its skin and muscle slip between my fingers. It is neither cold nor warm. There is no electric shiver, no desire to break out into song. It feels exactly like a mouse, filled with bones that mysteriously click and slide.

"Isn't he amazing?" asks James.

"No," I say and hand it back.

•

My roommate licks her butter-chicken-stained fingers and contemplates her empty plate.

"He's lying," she says.

"He's not lying, I saw it."

"Then it's not real. Probably a fake mouse."

"It wasn't fake, I held it. It's real."

"Then it's not dead."

"It's dead, it's just not decaying."

"What rubbish, how can it not decay? I remember once a lizard got caught in the hinges of my cupboard, couldn't have been more than an hour, fucker started stinking up the whole room. Small fucker, such a bad smell you wouldn't believe. Everything decays in Chennai, even if it isn't dead."

"Exactly."

"Mm."

And she begins to crack the sopping chicken bones between her teeth.

•

With the arrival of a new cigarette case and a tin of caustic foreign mints, there is less room in James's pockets for the mouse. He starts to leave it on his table like a paperweight and it is no longer referred to as Miraculous. I stuff it into my bag and James doesn't notice it is gone until the end of the day.

"Oh well…" he shrugs. "Hey there's this new guy down the street, he's got chili beef. Ten rupees." The thought of the chili beef makes James's fingers stretch and snap like pale, hungry birds.

"What about your mouse?" I ask. James shrugs and wiggles his fingers as he disappears through the door.

•

In the evening I watch my roommate pack her overnight bag. I don't tell her about Miraculous because weekends make her fluttery and she can't hear anything when she is fluttery. She disappears like a moth into the smoky, sulphurous Saturday night. I place Miraculous on the table and wait for it to say something.

"Were you sent by someone?" I ask. "Are you the apocalypse or are you just sleeping?"

The mouse remains silent. My hands begin to feel heavy and useless, as if they have begun to rust.

•

My roommate returns on Sunday morning with a deflated overnight bag and no papayas.

"You are looking at the stupidest girl in the world," she says and locks herself in her bathroom. She flushes the toilet from time to time to let me know she is still alive.

"He dumped me," she says. "Just like that. You know why?"

"No."

"He's getting married. Do you know who he's marrying?"

"No."

"Some chick from Mysore. His Papa picked her out for him and he said yes. I hope his balls fall off."

I pick up Miraculous and a chunk of its skin comes away in my fingers. My roommate bangs on her side of the bathroom door.

"What are you doing?" she asks.

"Nothing."

"Don't lie."

"It's the mouse."

"What mouse? You brought a mouse inside? Are you mad?"

"It's that one I told you about, the one—"

"Don't sit in my room if you're holding a mouse, are you holding it?"

"Yes."

"Well go outside and hold it then."

I sit on the crumbly stairs and watch as a large patch of skin falls away from the mouse's back, revealing a tiny backbone. It is the saddest backbone I have ever seen. I feel like I should glue him back together or hold a funeral service.

The tail and paws begin to shrivel into thin, grey flakes that slither along my fingers and disappear. Something falls away from the ribcage, crumbling into dust. I think of how heavy my bones are, how they bend and pull from the inside as if they are moist with decay. I wonder if they will burn completely on my funeral pyre or whether they will simply blacken as a token gesture.

Soon all that is left of Miraculous is a skeleton that looks like a lizard, poised and ready to run. I dig my hand into the soil of a nearby neem tree, feeling sand and pebbles surge under my fingernails. Before placing it in I snap off one of the paws—it looks like a tiny white glove. I will probably lose it by the end of the week. My roommate appears at the door and yawns.

"I'm going to make coffee, you want?" she asks.

My roommate is yellow and beautiful with the afternoon sun on her face.

She looks just like a papaya.

THE MARCO POLO MAN

On the way here, he found a beer cap that said Marco Polo Premium Lager so today his name is Marco Polo. He makes it very clear that tomorrow it will probably be something else.

"How does that work?" I ask.

"Nothing extraordinary. Yesterday I called myself Periyar."

"Ok. After... Periyar."

"No, after the bus service."

We are sitting in the worn and shabby India Coffee House, discussing the purchase of Chellam, the talking cat.

"So what does he say?" asks Marco Polo.

"Wow," I say.

"Really? Like how? How does he say it?"

"Like I ask him Chellam how do I look today and he goes wow."

"Every time?"

"Yes."

"Awesome. He probably has a mouse bone stuck in his throat or something."

"He doesn't eat mice."

"Sure he does. Everyone does. What about fuckle?"

"I beg your pardon?"

"Fuckle, would he say that?"

"Fuck who?"

"Fuckle, fuckle. It's my new word. Guess what it means."

"No idea."

"Come on, just guess."

"I don't know. A tiny fuck."

"Close. It's what fairies do behind mushrooms."

I think of a girl called Caroline, who refused to speak in English even though we all thought she should because her name was Caroline. One day I had heard her scream at a rickshaw driver "You jes' fugg*awf* min. Fugg*awf!*" I was going to ask what was wrong but I was scared she would tell me to fugg*awf* too.

Marco Polo places the beer cap on the table, which is scratched and splotched with tiny islands of water. I'm surprised at how clean the bottle cap is. I wonder where he got it from.

"Think he would say it?" he asks.

"You mean like right now? Right now, no."

"I could train him."

"You could train him."

"How much?"

"Five hundred bucks," I say.

"Not for free then."

"No. It's a talking cat."

Marco Polo nods and smiles. After he leaves I notice he's left behind the beer cap. I pick it up, feeling the crimped edges bite into my skin like tiny teeth. *You jes' fuggawf min. Jes' fuggawf,* I say to myself. I drag out the final 'f' sound, lazily biting my lip. I wonder if someone is watching me, if they think I look preoccupied and sexy. I spin the bottle cap on the table and watch as it rolls onto the floor and disappears under the cash counter.

Suicide Letter Is The Most Common Form of Letter

Senthil had two wallets. One was for receipts, business cards and on some occasions, money. The other one was for Amala's suicide notes. The first one she ever gave him was wrapped around his watch and said:

> *Why stay alive at such a cost*
> *When nothing's gained*
> *And nothing's lost*
> *And there's a lump on my elbow*
> *That looks like cancer*
> *Goodbye.*

He found her a few minutes later making tea in his kitchen.

"Well that's lucky," said Senthil. "I thought you were going to kill yourself."

"No," Amala said. "It's just a habit. I tried writing poetry instead but it didn't work."

Amala placed these notes in important but insignificant places like the bottom of his coffee cup. Sometimes she would mail them to him, giving him the envelopes to drop in the mailbox for her.

"Why don't I just open it now? It's for me anyway," he said.

"Don't you like getting mail? I love getting mail," said Amala.

Senthil kept every note she gave him. When he was on a long bus ride, he read them in chronological order and then backwards. On a good day, he liked to think they were love letters. On a bad day, he was sure she was already floating face down in the Cooum River.

•

Amala took him to her ancestral village because she felt it was important for him to see how decayed her history was.

"There are two reasons why nobody there will like you," she told him on the bus. "One, we're not married but we're sleeping together."

"How do they know that?"

"Two, you're a low-caste…what are you again?"

"Nadar."

"Right, you're a low-caste Nadar. My grandfather had low-castes working in our fields but they weren't allowed inside the house."

"So I'm not allowed inside?"

"Ordinarily, no. But my grandfather's dying so it doesn't matter."

Senthil fell asleep and dreamed that he was standing outside Amala's ancestral home. It looked like a mouth crammed with broken teeth. An old man was standing in front of him, a thick, handlebar moustache writhing on his upper lip like a black snake. He started to poke holes into Senthil's chest with a dusty umbrella.

"Stay away from my granddaughter," thundered the old man, though the voice seemed to come from the house.

"Fuck you," said Senthil, as the umbrella scraped against his spinal column. He woke up when the bus hit a pothole and snapped his head against the window. A thin film of dust had coated his mouth. In his hand was a note:

Only God says jump
So I'll set the time
We should have bought a bottle of water
When the bus stopped
Goodbye.

"You slept with your mouth open," said Amala. "You should never do that on a bus."

•

The ancestral home looked weary and abandoned, in spite of the people that kept shuffling between the slivers of sunlight leaking through the ceiling. On arrival, Senthil was given a tumbler of warm buttermilk that was so sour it made his eyes water. They left their bags in a room that was stacked with broken wooden beds. Then Amala took him to see what was left of the property.

"Some Dalits want to build a school here," she said. "They even asked if we were willing to sell. My grandfather doesn't know about it though."

"Why?"

"Are you kidding? Dalits are worse than Nadars. If he hears they want to buy this place, he'll have a heart attack. His head will explode."

There was a car shed with no car, stables filled with rusted bicycles and a field that was overflowing with holes and lumps of clay. Amala showed him everything like she was displaying someone else's scars. Lastly, she took him to a large, abandoned well—the pottakennar.

"There's still water in it," said Senthil as he leaned over and peered inside. Puffs of warm, putrid air gently clung to his mouth and hair.

"All the soil sinks in whenever they try to fill it," said Amala. "Six people have died in there. All women."

"Wow."

"The ladies in my family like to jump in wells. The men like to hang themselves."

"Is it haunted?"

"I like to think so."

They spent the rest of the day sitting on the only unbroken bed in their room. Senthil found an old radio and began fiddling with it while Amala sorted through newspapers, trying to find something to read. She finally gave up and rummaged through her handbag for a paper and pencil. After staring out the window for a few seconds, she scribbled something down and stuck the note in Senthil's pocket.

There's something I've learned
That you feel it
When they take it away
All these broken beds
Are bringing me down.
Goodbye.

"We could leave if you want," said Senthil as he folded the note into four.

"No," said Amala. "It's just the beds. I wish we could burn them and go home."

Senthil found a Sri Lankan radio station playing old Tamil movie songs. The announcer read a long list of dedications that had three Senthils, one Senthilmurthy, one Senthilnathan and no Amalas.

"I love the way they talk, don't you?" said Amala.

"Who?"

"Sri Lankan Tamils. It's like they're trying to sing but their voice never quite takes off."

They listened to songs about how the heart was like an unanchored boat, how the future was filled with promise but the past was filled with tears. Voices kept weaving in and out of thick clouds of static until the entire station disappeared completely in the middle of a song about the moon.

"Stupid Sri Lankan stations," mumbled Amala as Senthil switched off the radio. In the evening, a plump, sad woman brought them half a cup of tea each and apologized that there was nothing to eat with it.

"But we've got some nice fish for the night," she said, "Unless you've become vegetarian. In which case—"

The plump woman shrugged and smiled sadly. Senthil wanted to assure her that he wasn't vegetarian but she left before he could say anything.

Dinner was a silent and scattered affair. Everyone else in the house seemed to prefer eating in the kitchen and Senthil could hear the soft murmurs of their conversation humming around the kitchen door. Senthil, Amala and a small girl were the only ones in the dining room. The fish was soft and reeked of decay, even though it was drowned in a fierce and pungent gravy. Senthil decided to have rice with curd instead, though there was no pickle to go with it. The small girl sat on the opposite side of the table, gazing intently at Senthil with large, mournful eyes.

"Your niece?" asked Senthil.

"Who knows?" shrugged Amala. "What's your name?"

The girl shifted her mournful stare to Amala.

"Tell me your name," said Amala as she sucked on a fish bone, "or I'll toss you into the pottakennar."

The girl quietly got up and left. She seemed to teeter from side to side, as if she was still learning how to bend her knees.

"I think there's something wrong with her," said Senthil.

"She's probably drunk," said Amala. "Either that or she has polio."

•

The next day, Amala took Senthil to see her grandfather. He was asleep, breathing noisily through his mouth.

"We tried to give him a bath once," said Amala, "You know, just to see if it would tire him out so he would die? But he didn't—it's like he's staying alive to annoy everybody."

Amala poked the old man in the shoulder.

"Thatha?" she said loudly. "Thatha this is Senthil. You don't have to talk to him, just look at him."

They waited a few seconds. Then she lifted the old man's withered, yellow hand and pressed it into Senthil's face.

"What are you doing?" said Senthil.

"Let him feel your face."

"Why?"

"Just—"

The old man's hand dropped to the bed and Amala rolled her eyes.

"Well then *look* at him Thatha," snapped Amala. "Just open your eyes for a second."

"What's the point in doing this when he's sleeping?"

"He's not sleeping. He's just being difficult."

The old man's breath rattled lightly and then settled. Senthil caught a muted, stale perfume coming from the old man's clothes.

"He smells like lavender," whispered Senthil.

"He's very fond of Yardley. Come on, we'll try again tomorrow."

"An old brown man who smells like an old white woman," murmured Senthil.

"What?"

"Nothing. I was thinking that Polio Girl must be his great-grand-daughter. It's a shame you don't know who she is."

"I don't think anybody knows who she is," said Amala as she got up.

•

The next day the old man looked remarkably the same, breathing loudly through his mouth while a dying smudge of lavender hung over the bed. The Polio Girl was sitting in the doorway, scribbling on the floor with a piece of green chalk.

"Shouldn't you be in school or something?" asked Senthil as they passed her. He tried to ruffle her hair but it stuck to his fingers like clumps of damp feathers.

"Maybe it's not polio," said Amala. "Maybe she's retarded."

This time, they each held one of the old man's hands. Amala told her grandfather about how she had met Senthil, how he slept with his mouth open on the bus. Senthil noticed the old man's hands were warm and surprisingly soft.

"Thatha!" snapped Amala. "Either you open your eyes or I'll… I'll…"

"She'll throw you in the *pottakennar,*" whispered Senthil. Amala turned and stared at him.

"What?" said Senthil.

"Why would you say something like that?"

"It was a joke. You said it to the Polio Girl."

"Does my grandfather look like the Polio Girl to you?"

Senthil got up and made his way to the door.

"I'll just leave him a note, how about that," he said over his shoulder. "I'm the one fucking your granddaughter. Best regards—"

Senthil tripped over the Polio Girl in the doorway and fell, smashing his mouth against the dusty, tiled floor. He felt a trickle of blood collect on his tongue—his teeth seemed to be humming softly, like they had been electrocuted. He wiped his mouth and looked up.

"I'm alright," he said. "I think I chipped my tooth though."

"Well get up then, you're stepping all over the Polio Girl, for God's sake," said Amala.

•

Amala spent the rest of the day talking to her grandfather. Senthil watched her from the doorway; sometimes she walked around the room, speaking in English and touching the backs of chairs. Sometimes she would sit beside her grandfather, rocking back and forth, murmuring in Tamil. Senthil thought she looked very small and far away, like he was seeing her through the wrong end of a telescope.

"Well?" said Amala. "Are you coming in?"

"You look like you're at the bottom of a well," said Senthil.

"Is that a yes or a no?"

"No."

"Will you come in later?"

"I'll come in when he's awake."

"But he is awake. He's just being difficult."

"I'll come in when he's not being difficult then." Senthil spent the rest of the day wandering the grounds. He tried to pull a bicycle free from the rusty snarl in the stables but gave up when a wheel fell off and rolled away. He ended up at the pottakennar, dropping in leaves and watching them disappear into the dark water. Nothing floated—not even a scrap of cigarette foil. Senthil decided this was due to some complicated form of underwater physics which he couldn't understand. When he ran out of things to throw, he opened his wallet and sifted through the worn sheets of paper inside:

I wonder
Why everything's the same as it was
Why life goes on the way it does
Maybe one day you'll wish you had given me
Your black t-shirt when I asked for it.
Goodbye.

———

The light is swiftly fading
Angels wait to take me home
Even though Angels don't like
Hindu girls
Goodbye.

Senthil decided to write Amala a note. He would stick it on her forehead when she was sleeping. She would read it over and over again; whenever she saw him, the words would run across her eyes like subtitles. *Dear Amala,* Senthil thought to himself. Or no, *Just Amala.*

Amala.
What I want to say is
I'm being chased by insects.
I want to eat my cigarettes.

Senthil decided to write the note later, when he had something else to say.

•

That evening he ate his dinner with the Polio Girl. Her little metal plate held a handful of watery rice and a single, bright red chili.

"That's it?" said Senthil, looking at her plate.

"It's the only thing she'll eat," said the plump, sad woman. She dropped a teaspoon of salt into the Polio Girl's plate and disappeared into the kitchen.

"Well no wonder you can't walk properly," said Senthil. The girl dipped the chili in salt, bit the end and crammed a handful of rice into her mouth. Senthil began fishing out the chilies from his karakozhumbu and rice.

"Here," he said, placing them on the Polio Girl's plate. "I'm sorry I tripped over you."

After dinner he fiddled with the radio, listened to patriotic songs in Hindi and a play about dowry harassment. When he went to bed, he noticed a folded piece of paper under his pillow.

My grandfather woke up after you left.
He thinks it's 1964
And that I'm my mother.

He thought about finding her and asking her to come to bed. But he ended up falling asleep instead.

•

Senthil was sitting on the front porch of the house. The old man with the moustache was gone but he had left his umbrella inside Senthil's chest—he could feel it bob up and down each time he took a breath. Beside him sat the Polio Girl, writing something on the steps in green chalk. Amala was standing in front of him, dripping thick black water onto the dusty ground. Tiny silver crabs were swarming around her lips and eyes.

"They wouldn't let me in," said Amala, shaking strands of algae from her hands. "My own family!"

"You're not allowed in the house either? Is it because of me?" asked Senthil.

"Not the house, the pottakennar! I tried to drown myself and I floated!"

"But that's not right, everyone's allowed to drown themselves in wells. Even Dalit Christian lesbians who write feminist manifestos are allowed to drown in wells. It's physics. Or chemistry."

The Polio Girl suddenly stood up, teetering slightly. Senthil held his hands out to steady her, though he was sure he couldn't catch her if she fell.

"What does that say? What's she written?" said Amala, frowning at the green lettering on the steps. Senthil looked down at the words. They seemed to be shimmering, as if they were underwater.

"*Suicide letter is the most common form of letter*," read Senthil.

"That's incorrect on a number of levels," said Amala. "It makes no sense grammatically, for one thing. Furthermore, a suicide letter is not a thank you note. It's not a shopping list. There's nothing common about it at all."

Amala turned and began to walk down the steps.

"Where are you going?" asked Senthil.

"The pottakennar. I have to try again."

"Take them some flowers. Tell them I'm a wealthy Brahmin boy working in the States."

"That's a good idea," said Amala as she faded into the distance. "I'll take them some flowers."

•

Senthil got up early the next morning and walked to the tea stall for a cup of coffee. The road was dotted with crushed frogs, turtles and scorpions, all glistening mutely in the morning light.

"Would you like a Special Tea instead?" asked the tea stall owner.

"I don't like tea," said Senthil.

The tea stall owner grinned at him. Senthil suddenly wished he had said "I don't drink tea" instead.

"You're staying at the Big House?" asked the tea stall owner.

"Yes."

"Come from the city? You've come with Aiyya's granddaughter, right?"

Senthil nodded and looked back at the road kill. A crow was picking away at the remains of a crushed turtle.

"One Special Tea then?" asked the tea stall owner.

"No tea, coffee. One coffee."

"The Special Tea is very good."

"Don't you have any coffee?"

"No coffee, sorry."

Senthil made his way back, weaving carefully through the road kill. When he got to the house, he told Amala he was going home. She didn't try to change his mind—she just stood there, holding his thumb in her fist, nodding steadily.

"Are you coming?" asked Senthil, as he packed his things.

"Not right now," said Amala. "I still want my grandfather to see you. Have you got a picture of yourself? Even a passport-sized one would be okay."

"No."

"You better take some when you get back to the city then. You never know when you'll need a passport-sized photo of yourself."

"When are you coming home?"

"Soon."

"Tomorrow?"

"Probably not tomorrow."

Amala walked him to the gate but refused to come to the bus stop.

"Well?" said Senthil.

"Well what?"

"Anything you want to give me?"

"I'm not kissing you if that's what you mean. This isn't the city you know."

Senthil nodded and made his way to the bus stop. He watched as crowds swelled and stuffed themselves into every bus that arrived at the stop across the road. Senthil couldn't help feeling that he was waiting in the wrong place, for a bus that was going the wrong way. In front of the tea stall, he saw the Polio Girl. She had two grubby green mango slices in her hand, each one doused in deep red chili pepper.

"You keep eating mango slices like that and your stomach will fall off," said Senthil. She staggered awkwardly towards him and they stood side by side. A large, black thunderhead spread across the sky like an ink stain. For a second, the sun shone brightly on Senthil and the Polio Girl, then disappeared.

"You better go home," said Senthil. "Before it starts raining."

Senthil watched the girl as she hobbled away. When his bus finally arrived, it was completely empty. The driver was whistling to himself and the ticket conductor was sleeping on one of the front seats. Senthil sat behind the driver and looked out the window. The Polio Girl was still walking unsteadily home; there was only one mango slice in her hand now. He opened his wallet of suicide notes and pulled one out:

Don't forget me when I'm gone
Your heart
Will break.
Goodbye.

He thought of holding the notes out the window, then letting them go, one by one. He could already see them flying by his head, fluttering onto the hot, sticky tar like a flock of dying birds.

THESE THINGS THAT CAN HAPPEN

It is either Sunday night or Monday morning. Moths flutter like disoriented twists of paper as we enter a genuine Indian pocket of red spittle and highway magic. We both carry a reputation for missing the epiphany, for asking for a straw when the whole point is to drink from the bottle. This time we are ready; even if we don't find a bathroom, we are pretty sure there will be talking scorpions under the tables.

·

The sign is an angry city at sunset—important and undecipherable.

TOLAITELEADIE

"Wow," she says with genuine admiration, "That could mean anything."

This corridor has been specifically grown for the summer season and is thick with the scent of molten spiders and sweet tea.

"Brother can you tell me where the bathroom is?"

A boy with kohl-lined eyes jerks his head towards the sign.

"It'th written there, ithn't it?"

"But what does it mean?"

"I can't read Englith."

He slips beneath the curls of smoke and disappears.

"Did you hear that?" she hisses, "He lisped!"

·

We marvel at the phenomenon of lisping boys who go on to be lisping men.

"I never met a Tamil guy who lisped," she says. "Always thought it got eaten by the Adam's apple or something."

We practice lisping in Tamil, our tongues slithering like trapped fish between our teeth. A thick, black lizard waddles onto the sign and strikes a series of poses, hoping one of us will take a picture.

•

While watching the lizard pose, memories of no less than seven lisping Tamil men collide with all notions regarding the violent eating habits of the Adam's apple. Granted they all lisped softly, like stuttering snakes—this is why she couldn't remember any of them. The recollection makes her take a walk.

•

She returns with one of her sleeves rolled up.

"They have Pepsi, you want Pepsi?"

"No."

"You have to tell him now. He has to put it in the freezer for cooling if you want."

"I don't want any."

"He makes nice bread omelet, you want?"

"He who?"

"The guy making omelets. Hey are we still looking for the bathroom? Why didn't I ask him about the bathroom?"

•

Things would have been different if we were dying. Or pregnant. You need to carry a certain amount of drama before you can watch the universe spin inside a dirty steel tumbler.

"That boy? With the lisp? Complete put-on. He's going to Bombay next month to join the eunuchs. Did you see the bathroom?"

"Did you?"

"It's filled with coconut husks. I don't think it ever was a bathroom."

"Then what was with the sign?"

She shrugs.

There weren't any talking scorpions either.

THE DYNAMICS OF WINDOWS

When Prasanna looked at the Keerapalayam village road she thought of ants caught in a jar of thick oil. Sometimes she thought of wasps banging against windows but usually she thought of ants. The road neither dipped nor turned; it simply ran past the library as if it had more important things to see and do. Prasanna closed her eyes and whispered, "My name is Prasanna. My name is not Prasanna. In either case I am not here."

Last year the library had been the Keerapalayam Tsunami Relief Center and Prasanna had been the Tsunami In-Charge. She had spent her time looking after large cardboard boxes which she liked to think were filled with tsunamis. This year, the boxes had been pushed to the back and two metal bookshelves brought in, filled with Tamil translations of the Bible, water irrigation reports from 1972, and multiple copies of a book called *Where Are You Going, Young Man and Woman?* Prasanna became the Library In-Charge and her time was now spent sitting beside the window, watching the road absorb footprints.

Today a pale, ropy man strode briskly between the cattle and road-kill, his cargo pants and sense of purpose marking him as one of the tsunami volunteers from the city who had forgotten to leave. He entered the library and placed a package on her desk.

"We're not buying any encyclopedias," said Prasanna.

"My name is Kathir," he said. "My poem has been published in *The Macadamia Review* and they wanted me to keep these copies in my local library."

He began to unwrap the package, his fingers moving as if they were attached to invisible strings.

"The what review?" asked Prasanna.

"Macadamia."

"Isn't that a nut?"

"It's an Australian magazine. They were so pleased to have a poem from India, would you like to hear it?" He picked up a copy and cleared his throat.

Your lips do not interest me.
Your feet are cracked and dry like the earth.
Your ears flap like an elephant's
and you never have anything to say.
I am only here because you let me touch you
and your breasts are like
purple mangos in the sun."

Prasanna noticed that his lower lip was dotted with tiny violet scabs and flecks of pale grey skin.

"What do you think?" he asked.

"Well, mangos aren't purple. Has she been beaten up or something? Is it about domestic abuse?"

"I've seen purple mangos."

"Where?"

"Have you been to Goa?"

"No."

"I've seen them in Goa. Anyway, this poem's been published so it doesn't matter what you think."

"Then why are you asking me?"

"I'm not."

The magazines suddenly snapped and rustled on the desk, as if they were applauding.

•

The next day a suspicion took root in Prasanna's mind, something so aggravating that it made her shift uncomfortably in her plastic chair. What if the road didn't go anywhere? What if it ended under the horizon, breaking off into a wide, blue space that was filled with empty coconut shells? Or what if it simply came in again at the other side of the village? She frowned at the possibilities. There were far too many of them.

Kathir was standing in front of the library, staring at the sky as if he was waiting for something to fall on his head. Prasanna propped up a thick, dusty book on Rural Irrigation Techniques and watched him from behind it, remembering the purple scabs on his lips. When Prasanna was younger, her mother had said that bad girls bit their lips; it came with bad-girl territory, like letting your navel show when you wore a sari. This was why Prasanna had done all her lip biting at night, secretly peeling away neat strips of her bottom lip as she heard terrible things move inside her. She could feel monsters growing on her back, flicking their tongues and cursing her waist so that no sari would ever stay put. She knew she was doomed and people would call her Low-Hip Prasanna when she was older.

"What are you staring at?" Kathir called out.

"What?"

"What are you looking at me for?"

"Can you see me from there?"

"Of course I can."

"What am I doing?

"You're staring at me."

Prasanna could never remember the dynamics of windows. Night, lights on, people can see you. Daytime, lights on, people can't see you. Or they could. She sighed and put the book down.

.

The next afternoon Kathir's head appeared at her window like a runaway balloon.

"What if I changed the purple to green?" he asked.

"I thought it didn't matter what I thought."

"It doesn't. But what if it was green instead of purple?"

"What would that do?"

"Well, I thought about it and I realized that green mangos are more like breasts. Purple ones, not so much."

"Give me your hand."

"What?"

"Your hand."

His fingers were cold and pale, as if they had been kept underwater for too long. Prasanna glanced around to make sure no one was looking. Then she placed his hand on her left breast.

"Well?" she asked.

"What do you want me to do?"

"Are green mangos hard or soft?"

"Yes. I mean hard."

"Does this feel hard to you?"

"I was thinking more of the shape really."

Kathir looked like a rickshaw driver with his hand ready on the air horn.

"Maybe you should take your hand away then," said Prasanna.

"Of course. Sorry."

"I didn't know you were talking about the shape," she said. "I wouldn't have done that if I knew you were talking about the shape."

"I understand."

"Don't think that I usually do things like that. Because I don't."

"Of course not. Thank you."

Prasanna watched him disappear down the road, his head bobbing up and down like a coconut on a swollen river. Her ears were buzzing with questions that had no answers. Why had he shown up at the window instead of coming inside? Why had he thanked her? Why had she let him touch her breast?

"Why does anybody do anything?" she said, and the words hung in the air like a cloud of mosquitoes.

•

A few days later Kathir entered the library carrying a small plastic bottle. Inside it was something that looked like a piece of dried, orange parchment.

"I wanted you to see this," he said. "Sometimes a mother will conceive a set of twins but one will get flattened during pregnancy. It's called a vanishing twin. This is mine."

"This is your twin?"

"Yes."

"Are you serious?"

"Yes, it's my brother. That black dot would have been his eye. I wanted you to see him because he's the only family I have."

"What about your parents?"

"They're dead."

Prasanna wondered if he had flattened them and stored them in bigger bottles at home. She wondered if he would bring them tomorrow.

"Anyway, I'm going to Chennai for a few days," he said. "Will you keep him while I'm away?"

"No."

"I thought you would say yes."

"Why would you think that?"

He turned and headed for the door, leaving the bottle on her desk. His head re-appeared a few seconds later at the window.

"I was wondering if I could touch your—"

"No."

"How about when I get back?"

Prasanna thought she saw the twin wink at her from inside the bottle.

"We'll see," she said.

.

That night she dreamed she was sitting alone in the library. The twin had sprouted arms and legs and was sticking its tongue out at her.

"Do that again and I'll rip you up into tiny pieces," she said. The twin began to cry, rubbing its tiny leathery fingers into its black eye.

"How does he even know you were a boy?" said Prasanna. "What if you were a girl?"

The twin looked up and blinked, as if it was waiting to hear the rest of the story.

"If you were a girl they would have named you Kavitha. You would have married a software engineer from California. You would have had two sons with American accents so thick they couldn't pronounce their own names."

The twin giggled.

"If you were a boy, they would have named you Senthil. You would have loved cricket and been a state player. You would have neglected your studies in college and fallen in love with a prostitute. She would have died of AIDS and you would have grown a beard and thrown yourself in front of an express train."

The twin began to bawl again, piercing the air with a wail that reminded Prasanna of old ladies in mourning.

•

The next day was orange and heavy with the scent of lightning. Dogs howled for no reason and ants relocated in panic, carrying sprays of white eggs from one crack in the floor to another. Prasanna decided not to think about the road. Instead, she pictured herself dying in the Keerapalayam library, her mutinous soul slipping out of her ear while she took her afternoon nap. Her skin would fuse to her plastic chair and her body would be so furious it would refuse to burn on the funeral pyre. Nobody would cry, nobody would come except maybe Kathir to save a patch of her elbow in an old perfume bottle.

The twin was lying face down in the bottle as if these premonitions were too overwhelming to bear. Prasanna began to feel a little sorry for it.

"It's not so bad," she said, but the twin was unmoved. It stared at the floor as if it was contemplating something serious and permanent.

"You should get some fresh air, might do you good," said Prasanna. She went outside and tipped the twin onto the road. It skittered to the side and lay perfectly still, as if it was considering its options. Then it began to tumble forward, picking up speed as if it had decided on something. Soon it was shrinking into the horizon like a discarded plastic bag.

"The vanishing twin," said Prasanna and she smiled because she liked it when things fit that way. It was like hearing something click.

•

Kathir arrived at the library window two afternoons later, unshaven and smelling like the unreserved compartment of the Day Express.

"I just got in," he said. "Wanted to pick up my brother before going home."

Prasanna had seriously contemplated making a duplicate twin but she couldn't find any orange paper and the store keeper would not sell her an orange crayon separately. She later realized she didn't have any scissors either and decided that the matter was very much out of her hands.

"You want him right now?" she asked.

"I'd feel weird going home if he wasn't there."

She placed the empty bottle on the window sill and watched as his brow slowly furrowed. Before he could say anything she grabbed his hand and crushed it against her breast.

"Where is he? What are you doing?" said Kathir, trying to pull his hand free.

"I lost your twin," she said.

"You what?"

"He fell."

"Fell how?"

"He slipped out."

"What do you mean he-fell-he-slipped-out? Let go of my hand!"

"I'm really sorry."

"Let go!"

He pulled back and collided with the coconut tree behind him.

"Are you angry at me?" she asked.

"How can you lose someone's brother? Are you stupid?"

"How do you know it was your brother? What if it was your sister?"

"What the hell is wrong with you? How would you feel if I lost *your* brother?"

"I know, but I wouldn't keep my brother in a bottle like that. Or my sister. Also I don't have any brothers or sisters so—"

"You're crazy, you know that? How would you feel if I lost a library book?"

"I understand. It wouldn't really be my book because I just work here but I understand what you're saying."

Kathir was shaking out his hand like he didn't want it anymore. Prasanna got the feeling that something loud was about to happen and she curled her toes in apprehension.

"Where did you lose him?" he asked.

Prasanna pointed to the road.

"Which way?"

"Either way."

"*Which way?*"

"Or you could try that way if you are very particular."

Prasanna watched him go and figured that if the road ended at the horizon, he would fall off and there was a good chance she would never see him again. If the road came in at the other side of the village he would return; in fact, he would have to pass the library. It could happen either way, she thought.

Anything could happen.

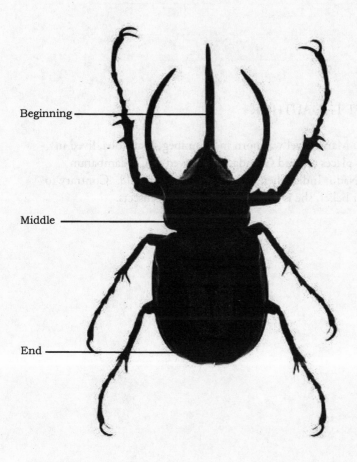

Beginning

Middle

End

Fig. 7. The Rhinoceros Beetle Seen as a Decorative Element on the Endpaper of a Short Story Collection

ABOUT THE AUTHOR

Kuzhali Manickavel was born in Winnipeg, Manitoba, lived in various places around Canada, and moved to Chidambaram, Tamil Nadu, India when she was thirteen years old. Contrary to popular belief, she is not very much fond of insects.